ISABEL'S WEDDING

Recent Titles by Pamela Oldfield from Severn House

ISABEL'S WEDDING

Pamela Oldfield

This first world edition published 2012
in Great Britain and in the USA by
SEVERN HOUSE PUBLISHERS LTD of
9–15 High Street, Sutton, Surrey, England, SM1 1DF.
Trade paperback edition first published
in Great Britain and the USA 2012 by
SEVERN HOUSE PUBLISHERS LTD

British Library Cataloguing in Publication Data

Oldfield, Pamela.
  Isabel's wedding.
  1. Canterbury (England)–Social conditions–20th
  century–Fiction. 2. Family secrets–Fiction. 3. Domestic
  fiction.
  I. Title
  823.9'14-dc23

ISBN-13: 978-0-7278-8151-9 (cased)
ISBN-13: 978-1-84751-417-2 (trade paper)

All Severn House titles are printed on acid-free paper.

Severn House Publishers support the Forest Stewardship Council [FSC], the
leading international forest certification organisation. All our titles that are printed
on Greenpeace-approved FSC-certified paper carry the FSC logo.

Typeset by Palimpsest Book Production Ltd.,
Falkirk, Stirlingshire, Scotland.
Printed and bound in Great Britain by
MPG Books Ltd., Bodmin, Cornwall.

One

I am so tired I can hardly summon any enthusiasm for this diary and if I hear the words 'Isabel's wedding' again I think I shall scream and who will blame me? One would imagine that no one had ever been married before . . .

Olivia glanced at the photograph on her bedside table which showed a small family group – two women (the younger one pregnant) and three small children. Sighing, she continued.

. . . I do miss poor Mother – even though I hardly remember her. I'm certain she would have dealt with the wedding brilliantly and enjoyed every minute of it but I am a poor substitute and am finding it a daunting business. When Theo was married last year Cicely's parents organized everything – I wish I had taken more notice of what went on . . .

Olivia Fratton smothered a yawn but decided to press on with her account until she could no longer keep her eyes open. She sharpened the pencil half-heartedly then continued.

. . . But at least I shall do a better job of it than Isabel herself whose nerves become frazzled by the smallest setback and who then finds relief in hysterics or floods of tears. I sometimes want to shake some sense into her but then she will claim that I am jealous. I know she sees me as 'on the shelf' at twenty-seven. Why, I wonder, did I ask God, all those years ago, for a sister when I already had two very nice brothers?

Poor Izzie. She is so young but cannot wait to be wed. She really should have waited one or two more years when she might be steadier (and might have found a better husband than Bertram Hatterly who himself is very young).

I fear Miss Denny is tiring of her tantrums – Izzie is constantly changing the details of her wedding dress and I suspect that when it is finished she will still be dissatisfied with it. Why do women as intelligent as Miss Denny decide to become dressmakers? Some of the clients must try the patience of a saint.

I have sent a letter to Aunt Alice promising her an invitation to the wedding but, although being our godmother and a very desirable guest, I think she may baulk at the journey from Newquay. She must be in her late sixties if not seventies. We shall see . . .

Seeking inspiration she picked up the photograph. Her mother had died two days after Izzie was born.

'Childbed fever!' she whispered and hoped that Cicely, her sister-in-law, would escape the same fate when it was her turn to give birth to Theo's first child. It was only a matter of weeks to go until the due date. What sort of father would her brother turn out to be, she wondered, smiling suddenly at the prospect. Then she frowned. Poor Theo had had no guidance as he grew up since his own father, Jack, had spent two years caught up in the final years of the California gold rush and had returned there in 1870 to rejoin a close friend he had worked with in the earlier years. After a few years neither man had been seen again.

'A pretty poor father you turned out to be!' she muttered to her absent father. The family had received half a dozen letters home and then silence. She picked up another photograph – the two men, taken on her father's last trip – arms round each other's shoulders, looking rugged and dishevelled with straggly beards and untrimmed hair. Aunt Alice maintained that they were no relation to each other but Larry and Jack were often taken for brothers. They were grinning, obviously very pleased with themselves, and Olivia felt the usual rush of irritation.

'While you were enjoying California, Father, your wife was upstairs in this very house, giving birth to another daughter and then dying!' she said accusingly.

'Two peas in a pod!' Aunt Alice had called them when the last letter enclosing the photograph had arrived, 'and not very edible peas, in my opinion! A useless pair! The less we see of them the better!'

Olivia sighed, baffled as always by the disappearance of their father. No amount of enquiries had found any sign of the two men who had last been seen setting out on, of all things, a fishing expedition. Olivia found it impossible to imagine her father killing anything and was glad that they had no stuffed fish hanging on their walls. She glared at her father's likeness.

'Mother said you didn't even like fish.' 'Too many bones and altogether too fiddly,' according to Aunt Alice who had known them better than most.

After their mother's death the four children had been considered 'temporary orphans' but to prevent them going into an orphanage, their godmother, Alice Redmond, had interrupted her burgeoning career as an artist and stepped into their mother's shoes. They expected Jack to return but he never did.

Only Theo could remember much about their mother because he had been five when she died. Olivia liked to believe that she also had hazy memories but these might well have been created by Aunt Alice (Ellen's closest friend) who insisted that they talked about their mother and kept photographs of her dotted around the house. She was not so keen to talk about their father who Alice felt was behaving disgracefully by staying away from his responsibilities.

'Do come to the wedding if you can,' Olivia whispered to her absent godmother. 'It would be wonderful to be all together again.'

Sliding further into the bed she breathed deeply, closed her eyes and waited for sleep to claim her.

Next morning, in another bedroom in the same house, Isabel was opening her eyes and stretching her arms, her thoughts already on the coming day's events. Miss Denny was coming at eleven for another fitting. Isabel rolled her eyes. Perhaps this time the stupid woman would have followed Isabel's instructions instead of claiming them to be impossible and making alterations of her own. They had chosen her because her prices were very reasonable but it had been a mistake and Isabel blamed her sister.

She sat up, hugging her knees, and thought about Bertram Hatterly, known to his family and friends as Bertie. Her face was wreathed in smiles as she thought about the forthcoming wedding but before long her anticipation was overshadowed by the thought of his mother, Dorcas, who Isabel considered a little too forceful, and who had originally declared her son too young to marry! Fortunately Bertie's father had finally persuaded her to accept the situation graciously but Isabel was thankful that she and Bertie would not be living too near them – they were already looking for a flat that was a reasonable distance away! If a bicycle or bus ride was involved, so much the better.

Bertie worked in a men's outfitters in Canterbury and secretly Isabel found this a little disappointing, even though he was promised a possible promotion to Trainee Manager which would lead to a position as Assistant Manager. Isabel rarely went into the shop because she hated to watch her fiancé being what she considered 'obsequious' towards the clients, his lips fixed in a perpetual smile, his hands clasped in front of him, his bright blue eyes exuding a kind of empathy as though the purchase of a pair of leather gloves or a silk scarf was of some importance.

Isabel would have preferred him to be a young doctor or a solicitor, with the appropriate dignity that brought. She liked to believe that he *could* have become either of these. 'But you couldn't wait, could you!' she muttered bitterly to his absent mother. 'You pushed him into the first job that came along, regardless of his future.'

Although no one in Isabel's family had said an unkind word about Bertie in her hearing, she tortured herself with the idea that they might discuss him secretly and find him wanting.

With a sigh, she threw back the bedclothes and slid out of bed. A jug of hot water waited for her outside the door, brought up by Mrs Bourne who came in daily from eight until ten thirty to help Olivia – her wages paid in part by Aunt Alice and in part by the money Olivia earned from seven hours a week as a reader and part-time companion to a wealthy but immobile neighbour.

As Isabel poured the water into the bowl on her washstand she made a mental list of things to do later in the day which started with a talk to her brother when he and Cicely arrived for the evening meal. Theo had offered to walk her to the altar in lieu of her absent father and she wanted to be sure he would look and act the part to perfection, right down to his buttonhole.

She had also determined to get a preview of his speech in case she disapproved of anything he might say about her. Her wedding day, she had decided, must be absolutely perfect in every respect.

Less than five miles away Theodore stood at the window considering the coming day and his own part in it. The auction house where he worked was a three-mile walk into Canterbury and the doors opened to the public at eleven. He, however, was due at ten so he had plenty of time before he needed to leave the house. Sighing a little he glanced down at the farmyard where his wife's father, with a bale of hay hoisted on one shoulder, made his way towards the stables where the two horses waited, hungry and fretful, for their first meal of the day. Marrying a farmer's daughter had been a piece of luck because Cicely's father had offered them one of his cottages at a very low rent, but it had needed a few repairs and in the meantime the young couple were staying at the farm.

It meant that when the baby arrived Cicely's mother would be near at hand and that was just as well, he reflected, since Cicely was as nervous as a kitten about the process of actually producing the infant. But then she was nervous about most things, poor girl. It was in her nature to expect the worst and to be delightedly surprised when a positive outcome gave cause for celebration.

'Poor little soul!' he whispered, turning to look at her, still sleeping at five minutes to nine. She was terrified of storms which involved thunder, frightened of mice, hated the heavy wagons which often lurched through the narrow streets of Canterbury . . . and was reduced to a shivering jelly if a snake came anywhere near her. Even a harmless grass snake had to be carried away and abandoned at least ten yards away, from where, trustingly, Cicely imagined it would not return. It had been this vulnerability which had first roused Theodore's protective instincts and had led to his desire to shield her from all things fearsome. Now, happily married, he intended to shield her from the worst her world had to offer.

Now, of course, deep in sleep, her face was set in calm repose and Theodore was reminded of the first time he had met her, asleep in a hammock, when he called at the farm to value several items which her mother wanted to sell at auction. Waking in alarm at his sudden appearance Cicely had slid expertly from the hammock – a thin young woman with a finely boned face and dark eyes which reputedly she had inherited from her maternal grandmother.

He washed and dressed as quietly as he could in order not to waken her and went down to the farm kitchen where his mother-in-law was stirring porridge with one hand and shooing the cat from the table with the other. The cottage Theo and Cicely were to live in was awaiting two new windows and the newlyweds were staying with Cicely's parents until they were installed. To his eternal gratitude Ann and John Stokes had welcomed the match without argument and treated him like the son they had never had.

Theodore greeted Cicely's mother cheerfully. This was the way he liked his day to begin. Quietly, with no surprises and nothing more to worry about than the usual hours at the auction house – although today he was frowning.

'What's worrying you, Theo?' Ann asked.

'Nothing much.' He shrugged thin shoulders. 'I still haven't worked out my speech for Izzie's wedding.'

She filled his dish and he helped himself to sugar and milk.

'She's given me a list of "dos and don'ts"! Let's see now – no jokes that might make her look silly. No suggestion that she is too young to be marrying. No criticism of Aunt Alice. No mention of Father's disappearance except a toast to absent friends.'

'I wouldn't call your father a friend – the way he's behaved! Going off the way he did. Running away. That's what I'd call it. Giving up on his responsibilities.' She filled the teapot with boiling water, set it on the table to 'brew', helped herself to porridge and sat down.

Theo said, 'Izzie doesn't see it like that. She's carrying a torch for him – always has done – and genuinely believes he will turn up one day. She likes to pretend he was prevented from returning, though Lord knows how. Izzie wants a happy ending.'

'Poor girl.'

'Olivia and I are resigned to the situation and Luke simply doesn't care. He's got his art, he's Aunt Alice's blue-eyed boy and he's got a good future ahead of him!'

His mother-in-law got up again, went to the back door, opened it and shouted for her husband to come and have his breakfast.

'It's Olivia I feel for,' she said. 'Given the best years of her life for you three and what's she got to look forward to at her age? Not that I'm blaming you. But how your father can sleep easy in his bed . . .' She shook her head then gave him a sharp look. 'He's never coming back, is he.' It was not a question.

Theo said 'No. He might even be dead.'

Her eyes widened. 'Now there's a thought!' she said.

Luke, the third child to be born to the Frattons, awoke to the realization that he was now free as a bird, having just finished his art training – a private course which combined art and the business of promoting and selling it – a preparation, Alice hoped, for the moment when she eventually needed to give up and pass the gallery into his safe hands. His 'Aunt Alice' had taken Luke under her wing and had found him a convenient boarding school which specialized in art, for which she had paid the exorbitantly high fees. She had recognized his talent many years before and was determined he would make a living from it in the way that she herself did and would eventually inherit the gallery she had developed in Newquay.

For a few moments, grinning up at the ceiling, he relished the memory of the flirtation he had enjoyed the previous night in the Coach and Horses, then threw back the bedclothes and, whistling tunelessly, made his way downstairs. Still in his pyjamas, unwashed and dishevelled, he picked up the day's post from the mat inside the front door. Even half awake, he was able to see that there was something odd about the address:

TO THE FRATTON FAMILY.
LAUREL HOUSE, NR CANTERBURY, ENGLAND.

He rubbed his eyes, frowning. 'The Fratton family? What on earth . . .' He looked for a stamp but there was nothing. Scratching his head he frowned and headed for the kitchen. How could it be for the entire family? No one wrote to all of them at once.

'Take a look at this, Olivia,' he said holding it out for her to see because she had a frying pan in one hand and a fork in the other and could not take it from him. 'Someone is writing to the entire Fratton family! It can't be anyone we know because *they* would know that Father is God knows where and Theo now lives at the farm with Cicely.'

'How odd!' She forked three slices of fried bread on to a dish and put a saucepan lid on it while she fried three eggs. 'Call Isabel, will you, please.'

He shouted up the stairs and came back into the kitchen. 'She's coming.' He glanced round as he sat down at the large kitchen table. 'No Mrs Bourne?' he said, referring to the portly 'daily woman'. Run off with a sailor, has she? I always knew she had it in her to surprise us!'

'Luke! What a thing to say. Run off with a sailor? At her age – and already married? They taught you some funny things at that art school. A good thing you managed to leave before they threw you out!'

He grinned and as ever his charm won her over. With fair hair and pleasant features, Luke was the best-looking of the four Fratton children and his easy-going ways made him easy to live with. Now he assumed a grim expression and said mournfully, 'Little you know about my time at that school. All those terrible beatings . . . and the starvation diet and the monstrous matron who—'

Isabel's arrival interrupted his scurrilous description of the boarding school. 'All lies!' she told him. 'You loved that school and everything in it. You were spoilt by Aunt Alice just because you could draw!'

'I didn't enjoy the cricket,' Luke said mildly, 'or the cross country running!'

'You are too lazy, that's why! Lifting a paint brush is all you can manage!'

In a belated answer to Luke's query Olivia said, 'Mrs Bourne has gone into Canterbury to the chemist to collect some medicine for her husband's cough. She asked if she might go and I agreed and said she might as well pick up some liver from the butcher for tonight while she's there.' To her sister she said, 'What time is Miss Denny coming to fit your dress?'

Isabel sat down heavily and rested her chin on her hands

and Luke said, 'Tut! Elbows on the table!' in a fair imitation of Aunt Alice in years gone by.

Isabel stuck out her tongue. 'You can talk! You would never have dared to come down to breakfast in your pyjamas if Aunt Alice was still here!'

Olivia set the eggs and fried bread in front of them and Luke poured the tea.

Before Isabel could tell her about Miss Denny, Luke said, 'Look at this letter, Izzie. It's addressed to "the Fratton family".'

Isabel held out her hand for the envelope and stared at it. 'So why don't we open it?'

Olivia plucked it from her hand. 'Because Theodore's not here and nor is Cicely. I think we have to open it when we're all together. It says "the Fratton family".'

'We'll never be all together,' Luke argued. 'Mother and Father are gone . . .'

Isabel broke the yolk of her egg, spread it carefully over the fried bread and ate hurriedly. Between mouthfuls she said, 'Cicely's not a real member of the family,' and immediately regretted it because they all suspected that she was a little jealous of her sister-in-law. In truth she had enjoyed her position as the baby of the family and big brother Theodore had always made a fuss of her. It had been hard to bear when Cicely came into their lives and 'stole' Theo's affections.

'Of course Cicely is one of the family!' Olivia gave her a sharp glance. 'She's married into the family, she is now Cicely Fratton and the child will be a Fratton.'

Luke said, 'Aunt Alice isn't here.'

Olivia shook her head. 'She is not family. Not a real aunt – that is just a courtesy title. She was Mother's best friend and is our godmother. Her name's Alice *Redmond* – no relation.'

Isabel's face lit up suddenly. 'I know what it is! It's someone somewhere has left us some money! You know how it happens – the solicitors have to notify people when they have been left a . . . a bequest! I think someone who knew Mother, perhaps, or even Father, has left us something in their will. And we all share it!'

Luke looked hopeful, wanting to believe it, but Olivia hesitated. 'It sounds too good to be true. But just in case you are

right, Izzie, we certainly *must* wait for Theodore and Cicely
because it wouldn't be fair if we knew before they did.' She
looked at Luke who nodded reluctantly.

Isabel asked what time they were coming.

'About seven, the same as usual.'

Luke grinned. 'And let me guess – we'll be having liver and
onions, mashed potato and gravy because it's Theodore's
favourite and Cicely doesn't care for it so her mother rarely
cooks it!'

Olivia had the grace to blush but changed the subject adroitly.
'We really need a bottle of champagne – just in case "the
Fratton family" *have* been left some money.'

Isabel pushed back her chair. 'But we will not be having
any champagne because we cannot afford it. We're impover-
ished, poor, without funds, penniless, on our beam ends . . .'

Luke said, 'I think we get the point, Izzie.'

Isabel was halfway out of the room before she remembered
her sister's question. 'Miss Denny? She'll be here at eleven.'

That evening, as soon as the visitors arrived, the family informed
them, in a confusing chatter, about the mysterious letter; they
settled in the front room in an excited flurry of expectation.
Only Cicely waited with something akin to anxiety. Theo had
already resigned himself to disappointment but the others were
hoping for good news of some kind.

As Theodore carefully slid his finger under the sealed flap
of the envelope, he caught sight of his wife's expression. 'Don't
look like that, dearest,' he told her with a reassuring smile. 'It's
only a letter. It can't do us any harm and it just might be good
news.'

'Good news about money!' cried Isabel. 'Just open it, Theo,
for heaven's sake!'

Luke held out his hand. 'Hand it over. I'll open it if you
won't!'

Olivia said nothing but her hands were clenched in her lap
and her throat was dry. She was trying to hide her unreason-
able sense of approaching disaster although she had not the
slightest idea what form this might take. To her knowledge
they had no serious debts, her brothers and sisters were well

and presumably happy, and no one they loved was sick or likely to die.

Theo said, 'I wonder why they have written the address in capital letters.'

Luke groaned. 'Open it and we might fin∴' out!' He turned to Cicely. 'Tell your husband to get on with it. The suspense is killing me!'

She looked at her husband appealingly but said nothing.

Seconds later the letter was being taken from its envelope and Theodore held it aloft in mock triumph. Instead of murmurs of satisfaction the room was suddenly silent. Cicely covered her face with her hands and Olivia drew in her breath.

She said, 'Who is it from, Theo?'

They all waited as he turned to the end and read the signature. His face paled. 'I don't know,' he stammered. 'That is . . . it says it's from Father. It's signed: "Your loving father, Jack Fratton!"'

Isabel saw that his hand shook.

Luke snorted indignantly. 'Seriously, Theo! That's not funny. Let me see it.'

Olivia said, 'I don't believe it. It must be a hoax. But who would do such a thing?' Her voice was husky, her eyes wide.

Cicely began to cry and Theo put an arm round her. 'It's nothing to worry about, silly goose!' he told her. 'It's just a joke but not very funny.'

Only Isabel was smiling. In fact, she was beaming. 'From Father? Oh Lord! It's like a miracle!' She clasped her hands. 'After all this time he's alive? I always thought he must be dead although I didn't want to . . . I mean, didn't you?' She looked at the others for confirmation but no one answered, still stunned from the shock.

Then Luke said, 'You didn't say that you thought he was dead.'

'Because I didn't want to say it aloud. Because that might have made it be true.'

Olivia said, 'Read it, Theo!'

But now he was frowning. 'Coming home after all these years? How long has he been away? Nineteen years – or is it twenty? He'd have been in touch long ago if he were still alive. I'll read it but let's not be fooled by it.'

Luke nodded reluctantly. 'I suppose you're right. It's too good to be true. I must admit I came to the conclusion some years back – talking to Aunt Alice about him. She was sure of it. Some sort of accident, she thought, and no one knew how to reach us and let us know.'

Olivia said, 'I just thought he didn't care.'

Isabel shook her head in disbelief. 'What's wrong with you all? Father is alive and well and none of you want to believe it!' She tossed her head. 'Well, *I* want to, so there! Read it out, Theo, or give it to me!' She thrust out her hand.

Theodore shrugged, gave Olivia a helpless glance and began to read: '*My dear family, I fear this letter will come as a complete surprise and for that I am truly sorry. Setting a fox among the pigeons comes nowhere near, I'm sure, to how you will feel when you read this . . .*'

He glanced up. 'He's right there! It takes a bit of believing that he would stay away from us for twenty years, knowing that we would think the worst. I wonder what Mother would say if she were still alive.'

Luke said, 'I wonder what Aunt Alice will say.'

Olivia said quickly, 'We must find out first if it's genuine before we start telling everyone. We must keep our heads until we're certain.'

Theodore peered at the writing. 'Is this his handwriting? We must have some old letters somewhere, to compare it with.'

Isabel gave him a spiteful look. 'You are determined not to believe it! Why, I don't know. Anyone would think that after all this time you'd be cock-a-hoop to discover that your father—' She broke off. 'Where is he? Does he say? He might be coming home and if so –' her voice rose almost to a shriek – 'he can walk me down the aisle when I marry Bertie!'

Olivia said gently, 'You mustn't get your hopes up, Izzie. If this is all . . . Well, just don't rely on this until we know more.'

Without prompting, Theodore read on: '*I don't know how the world has treated you but I realize that you are no longer children and I hope when we are reunited that I can explain my long absence, and you will forgive me for what must have seemed like my abandonment of you all. We will have a lot to talk about!*'

Luke said slowly, 'Does that mean that he expects to come back to England? To come home here? To live here with us?'

Olivia said, 'He can't just assume that . . . That is, he doesn't belong here!'

Isabel gave a short laugh, her face still bright with excitement at the prospect. 'Most certainly he does! This is his home, isn't it? He lived here once and now he wants to be part of the family again. He's never seen me, remember. I was born after he went away the second time. He must be wondering about me – as I've wondered about him.'

Cicely spoke up suddenly. 'And he hasn't met me, either. He doesn't know Theo and I are married and expecting a baby! His first grandchild!'

There was a short silence as Isabel stared at her, taken aback by the unexpected challenge, but before she could rally, Luke shrugged.

'You're his daughter-in-law. No denying that.'

Isabel gave him a sharp look but hesitated.

Theodore said, 'Should he expect to return here? Twenty years is a long time to stay away and then take it for granted that you can simply walk back in. Isn't that up to us?'

Realizing that the conversation was taking an unfortunate turn, Olivia said, 'Finish reading it, Theo. We have plenty of time to mull it over.'

Isabel cried, 'I shall answer it even if you don't!' She glared around her. 'This is my home as well as yours and if I want to live here and be with my father . . .'

'It won't be your home much longer, Izzie,' Luke reminded her. 'In a few weeks' time, after the wedding, your home will be with Bertie.'

Visibly shaken by this obvious truth, Isabel hesitated. 'Then he can come and live with *us*!'

Luke raised his eyebrows. 'I think Bertie might have something to say about that!'

Theodore said, 'I fear none of us will be *answering* the letter because there is no address but if you can all stop bickering I'll finish reading it. '*I hope it will not be too long before we are all together again and I can fill in the past years for you – and you can do the same for me. In the meantime, take care of each other.*

You have always been in my thoughts and I cannot wait to see you all again. If only Ellen could be there too. Your loving father, Jack Fratton.'

Olivia was finding it almost impossible to grasp as her mind churned with unanswered questions and with intangible fears for the future. She wanted to be thrilled and delighted, like Isabel, but for some reason the euphoria escaped her and instead the unexpected news weighed on her senses like an unknown threat that had suddenly materialized. In fact she had long since given up expecting her father's return and the family had adjusted, she thought, rather well to his prolonged absence.

Lost in deep confusion, she jumped to her feet. 'I must see to the meal,' she cried and fled the room.

In the kitchen she closed the door and leaned against it. As she did so she realized that she was still shaking and that shock was doing strange things to her. Forcing herself across the room she opened the oven door and, reaching for a thick cloth, pulled out the dish containing the liver and onions and then stared at it blankly.

'Oh yes!' she muttered and rose to fetch a skewer with which to test the liver. 'It's fine . . . Yes. It's . . . going to be very nice.'

She thought that if it was not nice it would be her father's fault and not hers. Springing such a surprise was unforgivable, she told herself indignantly. Closing the oven door, she adjusted the heat downward and straightened up. She stared unseeingly around the kitchen, unsure what to do next. How could he write so boldly, she asked herself. She took a deep breath and let it out slowly. How could he not even say how sorry he was for the way he had treated them? And the comment about Ellen was so hypocritical. There was not a hint of remorse.

'Potatoes,' she said dully, and collected some from the basket in the pantry and put them into a bowl and ran cold water over them. Frowning, she wondered uneasily if perhaps her father had been drunk when he wrote the letter, and actually had no intention of coming home.

Peeling the potatoes more slowly than usual, she continued to probe her own feelings and those of the others. Isabel had been immediately delighted at the prospect that her father might be back in time to escort her down the aisle. Well, Theodore might not object to relinquishing that particular task although Izzie would need to be very diplomatic about rejecting her brother so willingly.

The potatoes were cut into quarters and were soon simmering on the hob. Carrots were found and dealt with while she thought about Luke's reaction to a situation which, had he been a few years younger, he would have described as 'a bit of a lark!' Now, a little more mature, he might resent the intrusion into the family of a 'prodigal father' who might or might not see eye to eye with him – and might even try to advise him on his future! The problem was that none of them knew what sort of man Jack Fratton was.

There was also the nagging problem of why their father had suddenly taken it into his head to return to his 'long-lost' family. Was he in some kind of trouble in California? Was he trying to escape the long arm of the law? Even if he had done nothing wrong, was he someone they would want to live with?

Try as she could she found it impossible to remember much about him – except that he didn't like fish. No recollection of his voice. No memory of his smile. Not even a distant echo of his laugh . . .

'Calm yourself, Olivia,' she told herself and poured herself a glass of cold water which did nothing at all to lessen her anxiety.

Footsteps sounded and Theo came into the kitchen. He sat down beside her and reached for her hand.

'We mustn't panic over this,' he said, squeezing her hand sympathetically. 'By tomorrow it will seem easier to deal with. We'll sleep on it tonight and—'

'But suppose he just turns up on the doorstep?' Her voice rose a little. 'What should we do? We might . . . He might be someone we can't . . . admire. Then what will we do?'

'Mother loved him,' he said. 'He must have had some good qualities or she would never have married him. Cling to that thought.'

'But twenty years have passed,' she protested, 'and we have no idea how he has lived or where . . . or who he has lived *with*. Haven't you ever wondered about him?'

He sighed. 'I suppose most days I think about him only briefly if at all. He made Mother very unhappy. Aunt Alice says she tried always to speak kindly of him because she hoped he would one day come back to us – and maybe he would have done eventually. He must have known that Mother had died. Aunt Alice wrote to him . . .'

'But no one knew whether or not he received her letter.'

Theo opened the oven door and inspected the liver and bacon. 'Smells good. I'm starving.'

Olivia ignored the comment. 'If he thought Mother was still alive that makes it worse. It would be very cruel to abandon a wife to bring up four children on her own.' She shook her head, exasperated. 'All these questions I never expected to be answered. Now I'm totally bemused – not to say demoralized. I don't know what to think!'

'But if he knew we were motherless . . .' He frowned. 'Unless he was in touch with Aunt Alice and we knew nothing about that.'

Olivia, thoroughly confused, opened the cutlery drawer and stared unseeingly at the knives and forks. Then, with a jolt, she rallied and began to lay the table. 'I suppose we shall hear nothing else now from Izzie except Father's homecoming. She's determined to look on the bright side and I dare say we all should but . . .' She sighed then abruptly smiled. 'Fancy Cicely piping up the way she did! I think she's coming out of her shell a little which is wonderful.'

He laughed. 'No one was more surprised than me!' he confessed. 'It must have been the so-called mothering instinct – protecting the rights of her child. The first grandchild. It certainly gave Izzie something to ponder.'

After a moment Olivia said, 'As long as we all stick together. I mean we have to agree on what to do and say, as a family. And be guided by what Mother would have wanted for us. Aunt Alice said that a gypsy woman told Mother once that she and Father would one day be reunited – but she was wrong.'

'Cross my palm with silver!' Amused, he rolled his eyes.

'Yes. According to Aunt Alice, Mother believed in mystics and the stars and they both used to "read the tea leaves"!' She laughed shakily.

Seeing that she had recovered slightly from the shock, Theo thought it safe to return to the other room. 'Can I help out here in any way?' he asked.

'I can manage, but thanks for the offer.' She gave him a wan smile. 'Let's hope that maybe by this time next week we shall all be wondering what we worried about.'

'You think it will happen as soon as that?'

'We have no idea, do we? Why didn't he give us a clue as to when he might arrive? Unless he's still travelling and doesn't know when he'll be here.'

'Remember,' he said gently. 'We are all in this together.'

'Safety in numbers, you mean?'

As he closed the kitchen door behind him, Olivia reached for the cruet and decided that perhaps she did feel a little better.

Dinner that night was not, for Olivia, an outstanding success, because nobody paid the slightest attention to the meal she had put on the table. Understandably the talk was entirely focused on the amazing twist of fate that promised to return their father after a twenty-year absence.

At some point between the liver and onions and the apple pie the subject was their father's previous friend and partner, Lawrence Kline, and the new mystery was what had happened to *him*.

Theo swallowed a mouthful of pie and said, 'Aunt Alice's theory was that Father went over there for the second time because Kline offered him a share in his new enterprise – which none of us here understood although Aunt Alice thought it was financial – opening a bank or a loan scheme. Or maybe a business of some kind. She said Father thought they would finally make a success of the venture and he would come home a rich man. She blamed Larry Kline.'

They all groaned except Izzie who cried, 'There you are then! That's why he's coming home. He's rich!'

Luke rolled his eyes. 'This isn't a fairy tale, Izzie. He's not bringing a bag of magic beans or a magic lamp! Don't you think he would have told us in the letter if he'd struck it rich?'

'Trust you to pour cold water on everything!' she snapped.

'You've always been the same. When I planted all those seeds in my garden you said none of them would grow, just because I forgot to water them. You're a pessimist, Luke.'

'I'm a realist, Izzie. Anyway they didn't grow, did they? I don't recall any delicious lettuces or radishes.'

'I was only six! What did you expect?'

'A couple of beetroots would have been nice or a tomato.' He rolled his eyes.

Olivia said, 'For heaven's sake, you two!'

Luke grinned. 'I'm trying to save Izzie from a big disappointment. The most likely situation, if you ask me, is that Father and Kline are broke, the wonderful partnership is over and Father has persuaded Kline to get out of there before the creditors catch up with them.'

A heavy silence followed his words.

Cicely had gasped and now her eyes widened. 'Oh no!' She stopped eating, picked up her serviette and covered her mouth as if to prevent any further words from escaping.

Theo smiled across at her. 'Take no notice of Luke,' he advised. 'He is just trying to frighten his sister. He didn't mean it.' He fixed his brother with a look that spoke volumes.

'Of course I didn't mean it,' Luke agreed hastily. 'Cheer up, Cicely. It was only a joke. He'll probably turn up with a gold tie pin, expensive cowboy boots, a sack full of gold nuggets—'

Olivia interrupted. 'I shall write to Aunt Alice first thing tomorrow and see what she has to say about everything. I'll enclose Father's letter so she can read it for herself – and maybe read between the lines. She knows him well – or did. No doubt he's changed. He's twenty years older.'

Undismayed by Luke's mocking tone, Izzie beamed. 'I've had a brilliant idea! We'll have a party! A homecoming party with coloured streamers and . . . and balloons and champagne and Olivia can make an iced cake and we'll hang up a banner saying WELCOME HOME FATHER!'

Luke met Olivia's glance and laughed.

Isabel looked to her sister-in-law for help. 'Don't you think so, Cicely? It would be such fun!'

Cicely lowered her serviette and glanced at her. It was hard to believe, she thought, that in less than six weeks Isabel would be a married woman with a husband and a home to look after. Sometimes, she thought, being with Isabel made her feel almost worldly-wise.

She glanced at Theodore for guidance on this tricky issue but he hesitated.

'Shouldn't we wait and see what he's like?' he said cautiously. 'It's been a long time – almost too long – and Father might have changed a lot. Is it wise to roll out the fatted calf before we know how—'

Isabel glared at him. 'You're such a Jonah!'

Theo shrugged. 'We do have to face facts. The father we hardly remember might be a terrible disappointment. We might not like the man he has become. We have no idea what he's done or what he plans to do when he gets here. I suggest we err on the side of caution. There will be plenty of time to celebrate when we know him a little better. If we like him, that is.'

Sobered by his earnest manner, they were momentarily lost for an answer.

At last Olivia said, 'Theo's right. We should wait and see. There's no rush. We've waited twenty years! And we've got all the preparations for Izzie's wedding to think about. We mustn't let anything overshadow that.'

Izzie wavered. 'No–o but . . .' She was longing to revel in the excitement of her father's homecoming but also fearful that it might swamp the excitement of her wedding which was so near.

Olivia rushed on. 'You still have to tell Bertie the news – and his parents, naturally. I don't know what they'll think. And Cicely will have to tell her parents. There's plenty to think about.'

Had she said enough, she wondered, or too much? Her head felt strange and that usually meant that a sick headache was on its way. She stifled a groan. Often they could last for several days and leave her exhausted.

There was a long silence before Cicely leaned forward earnestly and said, 'A very nice meal, Olivia. Lovely tender liver.'

Isabel woke the next morning and decided she must be very careful what she told Bertie about their father's return. Sitting up, she plumped up the pillows and tried out a few preliminary phrases in a whisper.

'Dearest Bertie, I have some wonderful news to tell you! You will never believe what has happened!'

That sounded very positive, she thought, and it suggested that Bertie's excitement should match her own. He had to see Father's return in a good light and she must not allow him to suspect that Luke, Olivia and Theo were not entirely delighted at the prospect.

Or she could say something even more dramatic.

'Bertie dear! A miracle has happened! Our beloved father is coming home to us after all these years!' She could add something like 'We are all dizzy with excitement!' Would he find that convincing?

Perhaps she could add 'Do say you are happy for me, Bertie!'

But perhaps that was going a bit too far. On the other hand if she suggested that she was worried and upset about her father's homecoming, Bertie might feel honour-bound to try and set her fears at rest. Or he might agree with her!

She also worried about how Bertie would present the news to his parents – his mother in particular. Dorcas Hatterly, she had learned to her surprise, was inclined to worry – in fact Bertie had suggested that she *enjoyed* having something to worry about. She had been known to visit their local church in times of stress in order to pray and thus satisfy herself that no harm threatened her loved ones. Bertie would have to treat Jack Fratton's return in a very matter-of-fact way to avoid alarming his mother.

Isabel decided she would talk very carefully to Bertie about the letter. It would never do for him to suggest to his parents that the reappearance of the absent father was not welcomed by the entire family or that there were large gaps in their knowledge of Father's activities throughout the last twenty years. It must seem that all was well and that his reappearance would be welcomed.

She frowned. What *had* their father been up to for the past twenty years? Had he, for instance, fallen foul of the law in California? Another unpleasant thought crossed her mind. Had he been banished? Was that his punishment – to be sent into exile? Was that why he had been forced to return to England? The thought sent a shiver of fear down her spine.

'Surely not!' she whispered. Mother would never have married such a man – unless at the time her mother had been unaware of the true nature of the beast. So much in love that she was blind to his faults until it was too late! It sounded wonderfully dramatic and almost romantic but she did not think Bertie's parents would be impressed.

She frowned. Had he pretended to be a single man and married someone else? Was he a bigamist? Was he, by his return, about to heap more shame on the Fratton family than he had by leaving?

'Stop this!' she told herself severely. She was falling into the trap the others had set for her. Making her doubt her own father! But for much of the marriage Father had been absent so the possibility existed that her mother did not know him very well and might have been misled.

'No!' You're doing it again, Isabel, she told herself angrily. Father was and is a good man and you have to believe that or you will never convince Bertie of that. Jack Fratton was a charming man, adventurous, maybe not a family man in every sense of the words but an upright citizen. She tried again to find suitable words.

'Bertie dearest, something extraordinary has happened and I am the happiest girl in the whole world . . . and all my prayers have been answered!'

Yes, that was a nice touch, about the prayers. She would break the news when they were on their own. Bertie might be in two minds about it. He might even be a little jealous of the fact that another man was entering her life – a man she could love unrestrainedly. *A rival for her affections!* This guilty thought cheered her immensely. Yes, a doting father would be a great asset. Smiling broadly, Isabel climbed out of bed.

Two

That afternoon Olivia watched for the postman and caught him as he walked past.

'Wait, Mr Simms, please!' She rushed down the path. 'The letter that came yesterday, with the address in capital letters – did it come in the mail in the usual way?'

'Looked a bit odd, didn't it!'

'Yes but I wondered if it came via the normal route.'

He looked uncomfortable at the questions. 'Not exactly, miss,' he said cautiously. 'No. It came by hand, you might say, only we're not supposed to carry what we see as casual mail. But –' he lowered his voice – 'let's just say it happens sometimes.'

'Casual?'

'You know. Unofficial like.' He glanced up and down the street. 'Not paid for in the proper manner. See, this chap comes up to me and says he'll give me a tanner to push the letter through your door. Said it was urgent.' He shrugged. 'I mean, it's not the first time and it won't be the last. What harm can it do, after all?' He regarded her hopefully. 'You do someone a good turn and they slip you a tanner. Sometimes more. I had a woman give me a half crown once! Strewth, I thought! Half a blooming crown for a letter! My missus reckoned it must have been a love letter. Another time it was only a three-penny bit. It depends.' He shrugged. 'If it does the government out of a few coppers then serve them right, the greedy bug— Oh, sorry, miss! Greedy wretches! They should pay us decent wages. They think we can live on air but—'

Olivia interrupted him. 'This man? What was he like? Can you remember?'

'Dear oh dear! Now you're asking!' He frowned and scratched his head. 'What did he look like? To me he looked like an extra tanner in my pocket!' He gave a short laugh. 'Hmm? Let me see now . . . not a gent. Not dressed posh but not a tramp either. Sort of in the middle. Scruffy sort of hair. Bit weather-beaten, you could say.'

'Did he sound English?'

'Not exactly but . . . Well, yes I reckon he was English near enough. I mean, I understood what he was saying. Not a foreigner exactly but not from round here Not Russian or . . .' He shrugged. 'He was polite enough, I'll give him that. But I must get along, miss. Not paid to stand around gossiping.'

'Well thank you and if you think of anything else . . .'

'Yes. Might be another tanner in it for me, eh?'

'Yes.' Olivia nodded distractedly. 'Thank you.'

Once inside it dawned on her that he might have been expecting a tip and she rolled her eyes. She could have given him another sixpence. Too late now but maybe she would catch him again tomorrow. On the other hand she didn't want to encourage him in case he started making things up just to please her.

Minutes later, as she watched her sister hurry out on her way to see Bertie, she was trying to make sense of what the postman had told her. The man who gave the letter to the postman could not have been their father because that would make no sense – he would surely have come to the house – but it was possible that he had written the letter and given it to someone to deliver for him in anticipation of his eventual return. Maybe he was 'following on'.

But on the other hand it *could* have been Father from the description. The postman had said he spoke English *near enough* and that might mean with an accent – but not foreign. So not Spanish or German or Russian! American, possibly? And the man was polite. That sounded promising. She was assuming her father had been a polite man. Scruffy and weather-beaten? He might be both if he'd been travelling for days or even weeks.

She sighed. Did she *want* it to have been her father, she wondered. Tomorrow she would waylay Mr Simms again and give him a shilling by way of a 'Thank you' for services rendered, and see if it produced any further recollections. In the meantime she might tell Theo if he called in as promised but she would not mention anything about the letter's delivery to Isabel or Luke.

She felt sorry for poor Isabel who was now torn between her forthcoming wedding and the possibility of their father's return. What should she focus on now? Presumably her current concern was how Bertie would react to the news and how his parents would feel about Isabel's changed circumstances.

Olivia sighed. Probably best to get on with her letter to Aunt Alice who just *might* have had a similar letter, in which case they could confer – sharing their knowledge and deciding what was the best way to ensure a hopefully reasonable outcome.

Alice Redmond, unaware of the disturbing news that would soon reach her, was cheerfully absorbed in her gallery, talking to an elderly man by the name of Granger who had recently moved to Newquay and was likely to become another of the artists who regularly displayed their work in her gallery. He worked in oils on a small scale and she had four of his works on the wall already. They were more than moderately good and at the prices they had agreed on should sell successfully. Granger had confided in her that he worked quickly and mostly in his studio, from the various sketches he had made in the surrounding countryside. Alice was persuading him to be as visible as possible on his sketching excursions as it helped to be seen at work. People found it fascinating to watch artists at their easels and he would make friends who would talk about him to others. Word of mouth was very important.

Sixty-three years old and never married, Alice still boasted a slim, girlish figure and wore her long greying hair swept up on top of her head so that her dangling silver earrings could be seen to best advantage. A once beautiful woman, Alice now retained a certain grace of movement and a soft, fading beauty that men still found attractive. Something Geoffrey Granger said made her laugh suddenly and her eyes sparkled. This man, she thought, was not only a talented artist but he looked the part and would prove a great asset. She had no doubt that he would be able to persuade susceptible women to purchase his watercolours and the tills would duly ring in appreciation!

The future looked rosy, she thought happily. As soon as Isabel's wedding had been and gone and she was married to her awful Bertie, Luke would join Alice in her elegant house on the edge of Newquay and he, too, would be a fresh face at the gallery. Her stable of artists had never looked so promising. Luke would succeed at the art of *selling,* and being young, good-looking *and* talented would stand him in good stead.

'So when is your young protégé going to join us, Miss Redmond?' Granger asked.

Alice smiled. 'The sooner the better, as far as I am concerned,' she told him. 'The delay is caused by a family wedding which is due at the end of the month . . . or is it the end of next month? I must find out for certain as I expect to be invited although I may be tied up here and unable to travel.'

'Train travel can be very tiring.'

'I agree but how else does one travel these days?' She threw a kiss to another regular client who passed her on the way out then went on. 'Isabel, the youngest child, is the second child to marry although personally I think she is too immature by far. I really don't know what gets into young women these days. Hardly out of the cradle before they are looking for a suitable mate!'

He regarded her admiringly. 'It's well known in Newquay that you sacrificed a great deal for your little family in Kent. Most commendable. If I were wearing my hat, I would take it off to you!'

Laughing, Alice waved airily at someone behind him, but quickly returned her attention to him. 'I brought the children up single-handed and feel that my godson, Lucas, is to be my reward!' She laughed. 'I have invested a great deal in his career and I know I shall not be disappointed. If I were a gambler I would bet on it!' Alice gave a slight shrug. 'I always wanted a son and Luke is the next best thing. A godson.'

'He will be in a most envious position, I feel.'

Alice detected a frisson of envy which she had expected but she quickly shook her head. 'Oh no! He will have to stand on his own two feet and fight for his success the way the rest of you do! There's nothing like healthy competition in business and art is business – make no mistake. Luke will not be allowed to rest on his laurels or rely on me to push him forward.'

'That's very reassuring, Miss Redmond, although I never doubted for a moment—' He broke off as Alice again raised a hand, this time in greeting to an elderly woman who had entered the gallery, a small dog clutched to her chest.

Still smiling, Alice muttered, 'Oh no! That awful woman with the peke – or whatever it is. Nasty yappy little creature. The dog, I mean, not the woman.' She lowered her voice confidingly. 'I have never understood the need some women have to clutch their silly little dogs. They look like children clutching a favourite toy! It's pathetic.'

'Please allow me to deal with her, Miss Redmond,' Geoffrey Granger offered eagerly. 'I have a way with . . . with women of a certain age!' He raised his eyebrows humorously and she patted his arm.

'That's so good of you, Mr Granger.' She watched him cross the room to speak with the dog's owner who listened to him intently and nodded as he led her gently to the door and showed her the stanchion outside to which dogs could be tied while their owners were in the gallery.

There seemed to be a short discussion and then the dog was secured and the two of them returned to the accompaniment of furious yapping from outside.

Alice hurried forward, both hands outstretched in welcome, pretending that the awkward interlude had escaped her. 'My dear! How good to see you again.'

'I just had to see how things are going here, Miss Redmond. I know you have a very important exhibition coming shortly and I thought, poor Miss Redmond will be rushed off her feet so I thought I would call in and see you while there is still time.'

'How very thoughtful you are. But what about you? A little bird told me you had had a nasty fall and were confined to bed. It's good to see you up and around again.' There were several new paintings that might interest her, Alice thought, with a gleam in her eyes. The woman enjoyed seascapes and in a Newquay gallery there was never a shortage of those.

Bertie's mouth fell open when he heard the news of 'the wanderer's return' and for a few moments he was dumbfounded, lost in amazement at the turn of events. He stammered, 'Coming home? Your father?'

Isabel crossed her fingers, struggling to maintain her air of delight at the news she was sharing with him. They were sitting in his garden, sharing a jug of his mother's home made ginger beer.

'Coming home to us at last!' she cried. 'Isn't it absolutely wonderful? We're so thrilled. Can you imagine!? After all these years my prayers have been answered.'

'Prayers?' he echoed, momentarily distracted. 'But I thought you said he was dead!'

'We believed he must be dead,' Isabel explained. 'We thought that was why he didn't come back. It was a blow but in time we all accepted it.'

Shocked, Bertie was unsure how to react to the news. How did Isabel expect him to react? He thought rapidly and came to the conclusion that the dead father would have been the preferred option. There was no way a dead father could give or withhold his daughter's hand in marriage or ask the prospective bridegroom about his prospects!

'When is he coming?' he stammered, trying to pull himself together. 'That is, sooner or later?' Or much later? The prospect of a beloved father, prayed for over the last twenty years, suddenly turning up on their doorstep was decidedly daunting. Bertie felt that he had been misled in some way; that the fact that he, Bertie, was going to share Isabel's affection with a beloved father, should have been declared earlier.

'You could sound a little more enthusiastic, Bertie!' Isabel protested, pouting a little the way she did when she suspected she might not get her own way over whatever they were discussing. 'If he arrives in time for the wedding he will be able to—'

'I don't know what my father and mother will say!' he interrupted tactlessly. 'It will be a shock for them, won't it – as it is for me. What I mean is . . .' Suppose they did not care for her long-lost father? Suppose *he* did not care for *them*? It could be very awkward. 'I don't mean to be unkind, Izzie, but—'

'But you *are* being unkind, Bertie! Very unkind. Here I am as happy as a sandboy and you are spoiling it for me! I had no idea you thought so little of my happiness.'

Her voice trembled and he felt that tears were not far away

but he realized he had gone too far to draw back. He felt himself to be under attack in some way he could not properly explain and for a moment said nothing more.

'Why on earth, Bertie, should they *not* like each other?' Isabel persisted. 'Just because Father has been away for a long time doesn't mean that he's not a charming man and I'm sure he will have his reasons . . . No doubt he will tell us all about his travels. He must have led a very interesting life . . .' Her voice trailed off.

Bertie's mouth was dry and he reached for the ginger beer desperately wishing it was something stronger. Refilling his glass he spoke sternly to himself. Step carefully, Bertie, he urged. Don't let this get out of hand.

Immediately forgetting his own warning he asked, 'Does he say in the letter why he stayed away for twenty years with never a word so that you all assumed he was dead and even Aunt Alice took it for granted?'

She sighed heavily. 'All he said in his letter was that he was coming home. No doubt he'll explain everything when he arrives.' She took hold of his hand. 'Please, dearest, try to see it my way. Poor Father has not even met me! His youngest child! He must be longing for this homecoming . . . and we'll have so much to talk about. You cannot imagine how much this means to me!'

Failing to grasp this second opportunity, Bertie ploughed on as difficult questions crowded his mind. 'I hope he doesn't expect me to ask for your hand in marriage because if you recall I've already asked Theo and he said yes and gave us his blessing.'

Isabel *had* been hoping just that and she looked at him reproachfully. 'That's not a very mature way of looking at things. It would actually be very romantic and naturally he would say yes!'

'You sound very certain of that, considering you don't even know the man and might not even like him. If he takes a dislike to me he might say no and then where will we be? No wedding!'

At that moment his mother, Dorcas, came out to join them with a plate of biscuits. 'Everything all right?' she asked with a falsely bright smile.

Bertie knew at once that she had been watching them from

behind the curtain and had picked up on the fact that everything was not 'all right'.

Bertie looked at his bride to be and said, 'You'd better tell her, Izzie.'

'Tell me what, dear?' Dorcas had turned pale and now clutched at the string of crystal beads she wore.

Isabel looked at Bertie and her courage failed. 'It's nothing,' she said hoarsely. 'At least, it is but Bertie will explain it better than . . .' She looked at him beseechingly. 'Do, Bertie. Please!'

'He's your problem!' Bertie face had reddened.

'Not a *problem*! Oh no! Is this about the wedding?' Dorcas looked accusingly at Isabel. 'Don't tell me it's all off! Don't say you've changed your mind! I don't think I could bear it!'

His mother looked from one to the other and when neither could speak she said 'Well?'

'It's my father,' Isabel faltered.

'You haven't got a father, Izzie. At least . . . I thought you said he was dead.'

'That's just it, Mrs Hatterly. He's coming back from—'

'Oh no!' A look of horror crossed her face. '*Back from the dead?* He's come back from . . . Oh my godfathers!' Her eyes rolled up in her head and she swayed forward.

Both Isabel and Bertie leaped to their feet and just managed to catch her as she toppled forward.

They lowered her to a chair and Isabel propped her up while Bertie patted her hands and eventually they persuaded her to take a few sips of her ginger beer to bring her round.

'Not back from the dead, Mother! How could he?' Bertie's tone was irritable. 'He's coming back from *California*. At least that's what he says in his letter.' He found his handkerchief and dabbed at the sheen of perspiration that had formed across his mother's forehead.

Isabel, too, had failed to see the funny side of the situation and regarded Bertie with signs of desperation. 'We'd better help her indoors and you can explain it to them both.'

For a moment he believed he could refuse but something in her panic-stricken eyes made him decide to surrender gracefully.

★   ★   ★

At that very moment Olivia was opening the front door to Miss Denny. She said, 'Oh dear! Was my sister expecting you?'

'Isn't she here? I've brought the beads we've been searching for and she was eager to see them.'

'Do come in and wait, Miss Denny, and I'll make you a cup of tea – unless you'd prefer a cold drink. Izzie has rushed over to see her fiancé to tell him . . . to pass on some unexpected news.'

'Good news, I hope, Miss Fratton.' The dressmaker followed her into the front room and settled herself in her usual chair. 'I didn't bring the dress because it doesn't do the material any good to keep crushing it into a bag when all we need to do is settle on the design.' She gave a happy smile. 'I can't wait to get started. Any dress is a challenge and a delight but a wedding dress . . . Ah! That is always special. I'm looking forward to receiving my invitation and I've ordered a new hat for the occasion although I shall wear it to other events afterwards.' She leaned forward. 'I treat myself to a new hat for every wedding.' She laughed. 'My treat to myself for all the hard work I've put in! Silly, I know but—'

'Not at all! I'll just pop out and—'

'It's so good of you to invite me. You'd be surprised how many families don't include me. To them I'm just a dressmaker.' She sighed, studying her clasped hands, but then brightened. 'I do so look forward to the ceremony – I always cry – and the speeches and the toasts, naturally. I write about it afterwards in my special book. I have a book in which I put all the details of the dress and everything for every bride. Sometimes I just sit and read through it afterwards to remind myself and I give myself a little pat on the back. Metaphorically speaking. It gives me great satisfaction to know I've been part of it all.' She beamed at Olivia.

'I'm sure it does.' She wondered what the dressmaker would think when she discovered that the Frattons' long-absent father was threatening to turn up uninvited.

Miss Denny went on in happy oblivion. 'I have a feeling I know the design she will choose for the beads but of course I won't attempt to influence her one way or the other. The only consideration will be the cost and as we only have a limited number of beads that will affect the design but never fear, Miss Fratton. I know how to make them go as far as possible without looking too thinly spread. It's a matter of experience though I say so myself.' She gave a self-satisfied smile then glanced at the clock on the mantelpiece.

Interpreting her glance Olivia took a deep breath. 'I'm sure Izzie won't be long but she had to tell her fiancé about our exciting news. The fact is—'

Miss Denny clasped her hands. 'I'm looking forward to meeting her fiancé. Bertram, isn't that it? I don't know his surname but it's not my place to ask. What a lucky man he is. I'm just longing to see his face as his bride walks towards him down the aisle!' She sighed, smiling at the prospect. 'I always sit to the side so that if I can't see properly I can stand up and not spoil anyone else's view!'

'Very considerate of you.' Suddenly Olivia could wait no longer. Raising her voice slightly she said, 'The fact is we've had a letter from my father to say he is coming home and—'

'Well that's splendid.' She took a small screw of tissue paper from her purse and carefully unwrapped it. Carefully she spread it on the table. 'There you are – the beads! Not too small or they get lost but not too big so as to be flamboyant. What do you think?'

Obligingly, Olivia peered at them. 'Very pretty. Yes, just right.'

Miss Denny poked them gently. 'They have to be the right weight. It's quite tricky. We thought just below the bust. A discreet random scattering or maybe a curving line or even a spray. We thought silver beads originally but then Isabel saw some on another woman's dress and decided they looked too showy. If you don't judge it correctly they can look vulgar. I did wonder if silver beads would look right with the dove grey silk of the dress . . .' She positively beamed. 'Have you made the wedding cake yet? I expect your Mrs Bourne will be working on the menu, too.'

Olivia gave up. Perhaps it was only fair that Izzie should tell her the news. 'I'll make the tea,' she said firmly. 'I'll be back in a moment.'

In the kitchen she was able to grin. Quickly she laid a tray with cups and saucers, milk and sugar, and was spooning tea leaves into the pot when the front door opened, shut with a bang and Isabel rushed up the stairs, went into her bedroom and slammed the door.

'So it didn't go well.' Olivia murmured. 'Poor Izzie!'

She carried the tray into the front room and smiled re-assuringly at the dressmaker who was now looking anxious.

'Was that Isabel?'

'Yes. I'll pop up to her in a moment. This is such a worrying time, for her – so much to think about and she's only nineteen.'

'Yes. She's very young, as you say, but this should be such an exciting time for her. Her wedding!' She accepted a cup of tea and added two spoonfuls of sugar. 'If you go up to her and tell her I've brought the beads, I guarantee that will cheer her up. I can stay for another half hour and that will give us time to choose the design. I'll start sewing them on this very evening!'

Three

What a long day! I have so much on my mind and no one I can talk to. Things have not gone particularly well since we heard from Father that he is on his way home. I think we all have mixed feelings about his return but until we see each other face to face I doubt if we can tell exactly how we shall feel about him being with us again. I do hope we can like him and hopefully feel some real affection for him. I assume Mother would have wanted that.

Luke seems the least concerned but then after the wedding he will be living with Aunt Alice so however things have turned out here, he will not be directly involved. He seems to treat it all as a bit of a joke but then he never takes anything seriously. He has been rather protected throughout his life – cushioned and cosseted by Aunt Alice – and maybe that is not such a good thing.

Theo and Cicely seem to be weathering the storm. Probably because they are one step removed from it. From all accounts her parents have accepted the rather bizarre state of affairs with good humour – when told about Father's return after twenty years of being presumed dead her father said, 'That's nice, then,' and went on reading The Farmers News. *Probably more concerned about the price of hay or the next calf! And why not?*

But they have the satisfaction of knowing that Theo and Cicely will be living with them until the new windows are installed in the cottage and will then move into the cottage where they will be under the beady eyes of Cicely's parents and when the baby arrives that will take up all their energies.

Isabel worries me. After her visit to Bertie's parents she finally condescended to come downstairs again and talk to Miss Denny about the decoration for her dress. I don't know if she told her about Father. She was not in a mood for questions after Miss Denny's visit and went to bed early claiming a headache. I suspect she is torn between their own flat and living here with her newly discovered father. She even hinted yesterday that if she had to delay the wedding for any reason she would be willing to do so. What on earth does that mean, I wonder? I don't even want to think about it!

She thinks Bertie's family disapproves of the uncertain situation here but what can we do about it? We can hardly refuse to allow him into our home especially as we know so little about his present circumstances. We might be seriously disappointed — we might bitterly regret it. Are we heading for a disaster? I do trust not but what do we do if we desperately need to get him out of here? I'm saying little to the others but I feel it is a big risk.

It dawned on me this morning that in fact Father will not be 'returning to the bosom of the family' — if that was his intention — because the family is rapidly shrinking. Luke will be in Newquay, the other two will be living as married couples and I shall be here on my own. With Father, that is. I don't know why but I am not looking forward to it. Too many changes in too short a time. I do wish Mother could have been here. She, at least, might be looking forward to his return and would at least know what sort of man he used to be . . .

Olivia read the entry through but it did nothing to ease her doubts. The year had started so well with Izzie becoming engaged, and the prospect of a wedding had focused their attention. Now suddenly everyone was on edge and nothing seemed certain. No doubt their errant Father was imagining cries of joy at the prospect of his return but he might be sadly disillusioned.

'I wish you were still with us,' she told her long dead mother. 'At least you would be thrilled and happy to see Father again and that would help the rest of us to view him favourably and give him the benefit of the doubt.'

Olivia had written to Aunt Alice in the hopes that her godmother would have something helpful to contribute. She had invited her to visit them, before their father arrived, to talk about things, but she was well aware that the gallery now came first in Aunt Alice's mind and there was always a special showing to arrange, an exhibition to organize or a new artist to be introduced. After the years Alice had sacrificed to the well-being of the Fratton children, Olivia could hardly resent it if the gallery now took precedence.

She closed the diary and sat quietly trying to concentrate

her mind on Isabel's wedding which deserved her attention. She would check the modest invitation list with Isabel. At the last count there had been twenty-one guests.

The cake was already made – a large fruit cake which had been wrapped with a pink silk ribbon, dusted with icing sugar, and would be decorated with a single rose on the day. The simple wedding 'feast' would consist mainly of a large ham, a game pie, eggs in cream, a salmon and salad.

The wedding ceremony had been booked and also an hour reserved at the church for the rehearsal. As far as Olivia knew, the choice of hymns was still not settled but the organist had said he could play almost anything so there was no urgency.

Sighing, Olivia had just slid into the bed when a knock on the door revealed Izzie, in her nightgown and wearing a big smile.

'I must tell you, Olivia,' she said, settling herself on the side of the bed. 'Bertie has found us a very nice flat a mile or so out of Canterbury – which he can afford – and it will be vacant by the time we want it!'

Delighted and relieved, Olivia hugged her. 'That's wonderful news, Izzie. Tell me more.'

'It's on the ground floor and some of the first floor. The owners are at the top of the house and they are an elderly couple. It has a front room, one bedroom, and a sort of scullery-cum-kitchen with a door on to the garden where we can hang our washing, but they also use it and grow a few vegetables.'

'It sounds perfect for you, Izzie. I'm sure Bertie's parents are pleased.'

'Very pleased! They were getting a bit worried,' she admitted. 'We're going to show it to them some time and I thought you might like to come along at the same time – or later if you prefer. The previous tenants have only just moved out so it might be in a bit of a mess but we can go in a week early and smarten it up. Bertie thinks it would look much better with a pretty wallpaper and a quick lick of paint.' Breathless, she paused, regarding her sister with something akin to triumph. Gulping in more air she went on. 'So hopefully by the time Father arrives, we can show it to him. You didn't think we'd find anything, did you? Anything suitable, that is.'

'I was certainly getting worried for you but now you've—'

'Bertie says that if Father arrives before the wedding his parents will invite him for Sunday lunch so that they can see for themselves what sort of man he is.'

'How very kind of them!' So they wanted to see what sort of man Bertie's father-in-law would be, thought Olivia, and who could blame them? Presumably most parents would want to satisfy themselves on that point before launching their only child into matrimony. Not having enjoyed the benefits of parents herself, Olivia felt herself at something of a disadvantage. There was no problem, of course, unless they disapproved of Jack Fratton. But what could she do about it? Absolutely nothing.

As if reading her mind, Izzie asked, 'They will like him, won't they, Olivia? Because if they don't . . . I mean it won't get us off to a good start if my in-laws disapprove of him.'

Olivia stifled her own misgivings and smiled. 'I don't see why they shouldn't like him or why *he* should not like *them*! I'm sure Mother would have chosen a fairly decent man to marry.'

'But twenty years . . .' Izzie shrugged. 'Fingers crossed then, Olivia!'

Olivia gave her sister what she hoped was a reassuring smile. 'Trust me. Everything's going to be fine.'

'Do you feel it in your bones?' Izzie headed for the door.

'I do!' Olivia agreed, but as she watched her sister go she uttered up a silent prayer.

The next day, which was Monday, found Alice in her gallery which was closed as usual. Halfway to her desk she heard the letter fall through the front door on to the mat.

'Whatever it is, it can wait!' she muttered, pushing her spectacles into place on her nose. It was possibly a bill from the picture framers or an invoice for the batch of flyers from the printers advertising the forthcoming exhibition . . . or a reminder from the dressmaker for the skirt and jacket she had ordered – the pale green silk she would wear at Isabel's wedding *if* she attended the event. It was a long way to travel and she resented anything that took her away from her work for longer than a few hours but she knew Isabel would expect her to make the effort.

If she did *not* travel to Kent the skirt and jacket would also serve for the forthcoming gallery exhibition which would be opened by the mayor. Alice smiled with deep satisfaction at the prospect of his attendance. Persuading the mayor had been a really delicate manoeuvre because it meant that he and his wife would have to cut short their trip to London by one day and his wife had not been very happy about that.

She was also not very happy with the fact that her husband had allowed himself to be persuaded by 'that frightful woman' – a phrase she used in private to refer to Alice Redmond who, she declared, was suspiciously good-looking for a woman of her age and not averse to using 'womanly wiles' to get what she wanted – particularly where men were concerned. Alice had learned all this by a roundabout route and, far from being annoyed, was secretly immensely flattered. She knew she looked much younger than she was and that her charm was undeniable. Where charm failed she would use steely determination to succeed. Alice Redmond was used to getting her own way and very few people stood up to her for long.

She firmly believed that if the mayor wanted the position he must expect to make a few sacrifices, especially if it meant his name would be in the local newspaper, which it surely would be, and alongside that of Alice Redmond. The Redmond Gallery was well known in Newquay and for miles around and the mayor's attendance would benefit his career as well as enhancing the reputation of the gallery. Not that the mayor knew the first thing about artistic works of quality but his attendance would suggest that he did.

Alice glanced around her. The desk was strewn with sheets of paper covered with drawings and scribbled notes. She was trying to plan the position of each of the paintings that would be on display and it was not an easy task. The easiest solution was to hang them haphazardly – small, large, watercolours and oils – but Alice disapproved of this system and was constantly searching for a better way to display her works of art.

Some galleries hung several works by one artist together but this could look clumsy. Others grouped the paintings by subject matter carefully related to a common theme . . .

She sat back, frowning, trying to decide whether or not she could possibly attempt a themed approach, and then sighed. How different it would be when Luke was with her. The frown was replaced by a broad smile. Then the two of them would discuss the various problems and come to a shared decision. It would be time for her to teach her godson all she knew about managing a successful gallery and she would enjoy imparting her knowledge. For years she had worked alone, waiting for the time to come when her dream would be realized.

'And we're almost there!' she whispered.

As she pushed up her spectacles yet again she recalled the letter and, pushing back her chair, stood, stretched her back carefully and made her way to the front door, wondering what little 'extras' the dressmaker had invented.

Minutes later she was standing in a state of extreme shock, one hand to her heart. 'He's coming back!' she whispered. 'Oh God! The arrogant wretch is coming back! How *dare* he?'

All thoughts about the coming exhibition had vanished from her mind as she tried to grasp the enormity of the disaster. She moved slowly to her chair and sank on to it. Her heart was beating too rapidly and she could hardly breathe as Olivia's words leaped from the page:

> . . . *I don't know how you will feel about our news but I feel you would want to know at once that Father has written to say he is coming home! It is the very last thing any of us expected, believing he must surely be dead or at least out of our lives forever.*
>
> *We don't know what to expect and to be honest we don't know whether to be pleased or sorry that he is coming. Luke seems the least concerned . . .*

Alice gave an unladylike shriek. 'Oh Luke! Stay well away from him! He will cause you nothing but anguish!'

She read on, her heart still racing:

*. . . Theo seems fairly unconcerned but then he is no longer living
here and his thoughts are tied up in the cottage they are moving
into and the approaching birth of the baby.*

*Izzie is delighted – you know what a romantic she is. She sees
him as a knight on a white horse but she, too, will be married and
no longer living here so I shall end up on my own with him and
I am trying to think positively but cannot yet come to terms with
the notion that I have a father who, after years of silence (not to
mention neglect!) has re-emerged.*

*I'm hoping, Aunt Alice, that you can find some way to bring
the light of reason into this strange and difficult situation . . .*

'Strange and difficult?' Alice stammered, for once totally at a
loss. 'That's putting it mildly! It's downright disgraceful. How
can Jack imagine for one moment that he will be welcomed
back into the family after the way he has treated everyone?'

Slowly she read it through again, trying to imagine the scene
when they first read Jack's letter. Trust Izzie to get herself into
a flutter, she thought with a dismissive shrug. Silly child. She
was always very excitable and living in a fantasy world. Too
many fairy tales as a child with too many happy endings. Alice
tutted disapprovingly. Always dressing up and play-acting – and
still doing it! Much too immature to marry.

'But what's done is done,' she said aloud. 'I fear this story
will end badly for her if I know Jack Fratton – and God knows
I do!'

Olivia had said she was enclosing Jack's letter but had obviously forgotten to do so. 'Still in a state of shock, poor girl,'
Alice muttered unhappily.

Her thoughts drifted. When Jack had first announced his
imminent departure, Ellen had begged him . . .

Alice clapped a hand to her mouth. 'No! Don't go back there!'
she warned herself. 'It's all in the past. Best that it stays there!'

Not so many miles away on the outskirts of Canterbury, Dorcas
Hatterly regarded her husband unhappily. She was arranging a
few long-stemmed roses in a vase which would stand in the
hallway. Usually she enjoyed the task but today her mind was
on other things – on one thing in particular.

Wesley Hatterly sat on the third step of the staircase, looking wary and confused.

'The thing is, dear,' his wife explained, 'that we must give this affair proper thought. We know nothing about this man who is going to be our son's father-in-law and if we know nothing, we are at a great disadvantage. Supposing he is not at all desirable. He will be grandfather to Bertie's children!'

'That could be . . . that is, he might not be unsuitable. Aren't you looking on the black side, dear?'

She gave him a withering look. 'I grant you he may appear to be a suitable person *now* but suppose we discover, when it's too late, that he has an unsavoury past. Then what will we do? Should we allow our only child to marry in haste and discover serious problems later on? Do we want our future grandchildren to be scarred by their association with him?'

'But Bertie and Isabel are already betrothed, Dorcas. We can't expect Bertie to break off the engagement on the off-chance that we don't like him. It would be all over Canterbury in a moment and if he is a charming man we would look very foolish.'

Dorcas glared at the roses, snatched them from the vase and took up the secateurs. Distractedly she began to cut two inches from each stem. 'The alternative might be to watch our son's marriage damaged by revelations from his father-in-law's past! The man might have another wife back in America!'

'Another . . .? Oh my Lord!' Shocked, Wesley stared up at her pale face. 'Do you know something I don't know?'

'Only hints. Snippets of gossip. Whispers of rows within the Fratton family – before he left the second time, that is.' She lowered her voice. 'The way I heard it, the postman arrived at their house one day and heard a big argument going on and he took a quick glance through the letterbox and saw one of the women rushing up the stairs sobbing and—'

'The postman has no right to—'

'Don't interrupt, dear! He claims he was worried that things might go too far.'

He blinked. 'What do you mean? Fisticuffs?'

Dorcas shrugged. 'Let's just say these things do happen and not just among the lower classes.'

'But Isabel was only a child then. Maybe not even born! How could she be involved in a family quarrel?'

'I'm not saying she was involved. I'm saying that things were going on in the family and we don't know what they were. Nor do we know why the father went rushing off the way he did – to America, of all places. It was a mystery then and it still is.'

'And all I'm saying, Dorcas, is that it has nothing to do with Isabel.' Wesley dug his heels in. He had always liked Isabel even though she was a bit of a scatterbrain. She was young and she would settle down. 'She cannot be to blame for anything that happened before she was born!'

She sighed heavily. 'Poor Wesley, you are too innocent. Ever the optimist! You cannot grasp the problem, can you; cannot see ahead. I'm not blaming Isabel. I'm trying to protect our son from what might be a disastrous marriage. And please don't say we must hope for the best. That is not good enough for our Bertie.'

Her husband fell silent, thinking hard. 'You said one of the women was rushing up the stairs. Surely there was only one woman there. Ellen Fratton.'

Dorcas shook her head. 'You're forgetting the godmother who eventually brought them up. She often stayed with them. Alice Redmond – Ellen's best friend.' She sighed. 'Oh why did Bertie have to choose a young woman like Isabel? I've nothing against her as such but she hasn't lived a normal life.'

'Steady on, dear!' Wesley protested. That's a bit hard.'

'I'm being practical, dear. I'm facing facts. A young woman learns how to be a mother by sitting at her own mother's knee and poor Isabel has never known a mother's love. She has had no one to learn from.'

'But now she has you, dear.'

'It's not the same.'

'And they had the godmother.'

Dorcas rolled her eyes. 'I wouldn't expect a man to understand the nuances of the matter but never mind.' She gathered the roses into one hand and jammed them back into the vase. 'Oh no!' she wailed, her voice trembling. 'They're too short now.'

After a short silence Wesley leaned forward, clasping his hands, his elbows on his thighs. He said cautiously, 'I thought you liked Isabel. I thought you approved of her.'

'I did. I do.'

'You don't sound very sure. Whatever would Bertie think if he could hear you?'

She fiddled with the roses, not meeting his eyes. 'Maybe Bertie is also having second thoughts. I mean, this wretched business with the father rather changes things, don't you think?' She turned to him abruptly. 'I think you must have a word with him, dear. Just to reassure us that his feelings haven't changed towards her. He is so loyal – he may not wish to say anything.'

He straightened up. 'Oh no! Not me! It's your idea. If anyone has to say anything it must be you.'

'You're his father! It's your duty.'

'Jack Fratton might be a very charming man!' he said desperately. 'He obviously has a conscience or he wouldn't be coming back to them. His good instincts have got the better of him and . . . and maybe he regrets his past mistakes. He may be longing to put matters right.' He regarded his wife hopefully.

'And he may not!' She snatched the rose from the vase for the second time. 'I do so hate roses!'

He stared at her. 'They're your favourites, Dorcas! Always have been. Do you remember when I sent you a dozen red roses and they were—'

'Not these. They are so . . . so *damned* intractable!'

'Dorcas!' Now he was definitely alarmed. He had never heard his wife swear.

Turning abruptly, Dorcas walked back towards the kitchen, her face crumpled, her shoulders slightly bowed, and he knew that within minutes she would be in tears. He stood up slowly, one hand on the banisters. Maybe she was right and maybe not but a few words with Bertie, tactfully chosen, might help to clear the air and could certainly do no harm.

Two days later, just before midday in a cheap rooming-house in Dover a man stood in front of a small swing mirror, staring fixedly at his own reflection while countless questions filled his mind and gave him serious concern. How would he look to the family, he wondered. Weird in some way? Foreign? He shook his head unhappily. Would they be waiting with open arms or would they be deeply resentful?

'They're not going to welcome you!' he muttered unhappily. 'Hardly going to hang up the bunting!'

Why should they? Their father had abandoned them twenty years ago, near as dammit, so what right did he have to turn up uninvited and expect to be greeted with open arms? There would be no banner saying 'WELCOME HOME'! The more he thought about it, the more he admitted that this journey had been ill-considered at best, and stupid and utterly futile at worst.

He ran a hand over his short beard and wondered whether to shave it off. Once it had been a bright sandy colour but now it was mostly grey. Not that it mattered. None of them would remember what Jack Fratton looked like – except maybe from an old photograph – and obviously he would have changed his appearance over the years. But he looked like a roughneck. Would they care or would they be totally uninterested? Hostile, even. If they were, he would understand.

Ever since deciding to return to England he had clung to the idea of a reunion and had even imagined a smiling family, with forgiveness in their hearts, rushing down the path to greet him. Now he was within a few hours' travel from Canterbury this vision was fading as the doubts crowded in.

He sighed deeply, running his fingers over his moustache. Should the moustache go? Maybe the combination of beard and moustache was altogether too American. Too foreign-looking.

'Hell!' he muttered, turning from the mirror and throwing himself on to his back on the unmade bed. Maybe if they did not consider him worthy of the word Father he could ask them to call him Jack. They might find that easier.

'Hi there! I'm Jack!' he said, smiling up at the ceiling. It sounded unconvincing even to *his* ears. 'Goddam!' Choked, he closed his eyes. How had he ever thought that this was a good idea? For a moment he struggled with his emotions, fighting against the urge to give up the whole ill-considered enterprise. But this family was all there was of Ellen. Win or lose he had to go on. He had to at least see her children and know how they were faring. Sitting up, he swung his legs to the floor and turned to stare out of the window.

He wondered if the family had told anyone he was coming or if they were too ashamed or confused to talk about him. He crossed his fingers. Thank God Alice Redmond would not be around. She had been much older than Ellen and would be long gone! Poor Alice. Jack Fratton had broken her heart and she had retaliated. Did he condone her behaviour? No, but he understood where her hatred came from.

Two days later Theo turned up for work and began the usual task of taking notes on the items which would be published in the next brochure. The new items up for auction were set out on a trestle table and Michael Rawley, the senior assessor, was holding a piece of pottery upside down and peering beneath it for the maker's mark.

'Definitely late eighteenth century,' he said aloud and waited for his trainee to note it in the ledger. Rawley was in his fifties with a bulging waistline and a small round face below untidy grey hair. 'Biscuit barrel with worn raffia handle. Nice colours but a few small scratches round the rim and the lid has been repaired . . .'

He would set a price later. The present task was to describe the objects for Theo to note. He moved on, reaching for a pewter jug. He lifted the lid and peered inside, tutting in disapproval as he did so. 'Someone's tried to clean it up,' he grumbled, showing the item to Theodore. 'Ruined it. Even scoured the inside. Would you believe it?' He shook his head. 'So what did you think of our Miss Fawcett's little book? Didn't know she had it in her, did you? I certainly didn't. She kept that quiet. *Dolls Through The Ages*, eh?' He shrugged. 'I daren't tell my wife. She's been nagging me for years to produce a book.'

Theodore nodded eagerly. 'I thought it was excellent. Very clever of her. She even did the sketches, apparently. Hidden talents!'

They laughed; then the older man hesitated and turned to

Theodore. 'I've been hearing some odd rumours, Fratton. About your long-lost father. Rather far-fetched, I fancied, but my wife insisted she'd heard the selfsame gossip. Any truth in the story?'

Theodore groaned inwardly and drew a deep breath. He had been expecting the news to leak out somehow. 'If you mean our father's return to England, they are right. We had a letter some days ago. A bit of a shock, to say the least! We gave up on him years ago and thought, after no word for twenty years, he must surely be dead. And without Mother to keep our hopes up . . .' He left the sentence unfinished.

Rawley's eyes widened. 'You mean it's true? Coming home again after all these years? Well I'm blessed! Wonders will never cease!' He peered at Theodore through his small round spectacles. 'That will be an event, that will! The prodigal father! Hah!' He slapped his right leg which was his way of showing excitement. 'He must have quite a tale to tell, your father! Bit of a wild place, America, or so they say. California, wasn't it?'

Theo nodded, trying to look at ease with the subject and failing. 'I expect we shall hear all about it when he arrives. We're still trying to recover from the shock, as you might imagine, and we were already busy with Isabel's wedding.' He was hoping to divert Rawley's attention but failed again. 'My younger sister became engaged . . .'

'So when is he arriving, this wanderer?'

He was obviously not interested in the wedding, thought Theodore. That would mortify Isabel, if she knew. 'He didn't say. The letter came by hand so we imagine he is travelling and doesn't yet know when he will reach us. Isabel had asked me to walk her down the aisle and I was working on my speech when . . .'

But suddenly his companion had lost interest. He picked up a small portrait and peered at it then pulled a magnifying glass from his pocket and gave it a closer scrutiny. 'Lovely work. Very fine,' he muttered, 'and see the young woman's expression, so delicately done. Exquisite. Pity there's no signature although it might be on the back but I'll have to get the back off and these things are so fragile. I'm always afraid they will fall to pieces and we can't have that! I'll ask Mr Pope when he comes in. He knows more about miniatures than I do.' He glanced up at Theodore. 'You could write a book, Fratton. You can't be beaten by a slip of a girl! You know quite a bit about barometers and suchlike. Remember that one you discovered last year. French wasn't it?'

'Yes, but that was a bit of a fluke.'

'A fluke? Nonsense. It was nothing of the sort. You've got a good eye, young man. Clocks, too. Start now and take your time over it. Ever thought about it?'

'I haven't, but thank you. Maybe I should give it a try.' Theodore found himself blushing at the older man's compliment.

'Good! No time like the present. Start tomorrow.' He laughed.

Theodore hid his panic. 'Just at the moment I could not start on anything like that,' he protested weakly. 'We have a baby on the way and Isabel's wedding rushing towards us – not to mention Father!'

'Rather thrown a spoke in the wheel, has he? Never mind. But why not set yourself a date? For the book, I mean. Say, make a start by Christmas.'

'I'll certainly think about it,' Theo stammered, flustered by so much attention.

'Tell you what – I'll help you with it here and there when I have a moment. Impress your old man, eh?' He chuckled. 'Is it a deal, Fratton?'

'A deal? Oh well . . . Yes, I suppose so.' Was he really saying this? Was he really committing himself to compiling a book? 'Thank you! That's very generous of you, Mr Rawley.' Theodore shook the meaty hand outstretched towards him. 'I truly appreciate your offer. Wait until I tell Cicely!'

In fact he dreaded telling her. The idea of him stepping off the path of their life together – of venturing into the wider world outside Canterbury – would thoroughly alarm her. The prospect of her husband setting foot in London to become involved in the world of book publishing would certainly unnerve her. Theo gave a wry smile. What was he saying? Who was he fooling? The whole book idea unnerved *him*!

★　　★　　★

That same day Alice's letter arrived, and far from reassuring Olivia it had the opposite effect. She read the four elegantly written pages with a growing dismay which bordered on panic and decided that she must put it aside until she felt strong enough to reread it and share it with the other family members. Alone in the house, she felt as though a huge weight was settling upon her and the responsibility of having to deal with it was giving her no peace. After a few minutes, however, she knew that the longer she delayed action the worse it would be and forced herself to reread it:

> *My dear Olivia,*
>
> *You forgot to include your father's letter but you told me enough in your own letter and it has quite simply ruined my day. At the ripe old age of sixty-nine . . .*

Olivia wondered if this was really her godmother's age. She had always been very secretive about her age.

> *. . . I am too old to deal with such unwelcome news which has come as a great shock. I shall cross my fingers that I am still able to reach seventy!*
>
> *But to be serious, you all have my sincere commiserations for what has happened – or is about to happen. Sadly I am at a loss to offer anything useful in the way of advice except to warn you to be very wary of the man. My hazy memories of that unhappy time when your father chose to head for California instead of staying to care for his family will never quite leave me and the disastrous effect it had on poor Ellen remains clear to this day. Quite simply the wretch broke her heart. I would go so far as to say that grief contributed to her early death.*
>
> *How very like the Jack Fratton I remember – expecting you all to rush to his side now that he has decided to return. I imagine that even Theo has no real memory of his father – you were all so very young when he left and Jack, of course, has never even seen Isabel . . .*

Olivia sighed heavily. She had been relying on Alice to somehow show her the way to reconciliation but the more she read, the less she could imagine ever feeling magnanimous towards her father.

> *. . . I can only suggest that you wait and see. He may have changed his ways and if so you may be able to discover a nicer Jack Fratton than the one I remember. (The moon may be made of green cheese!) Of the two friends, Jack and Larry, the latter would have made a perfect husband for Ellen but sadly she changed her mind at the last moment. A tragic mistake.*
>
> *No point in crying over spilt milk, I hear you say. True. What happened, happened.*
>
> *Do please send me an invitation to Isabel's wedding but it is very close now and as things are here at the moment (hectically busy) I doubt I shall feel able to desert the gallery, nor will I be up to the journey. I know you will understand that at my age I have to protect my health. All good wishes . . .*
>
> *Your loving Aunt Alice*

Frowning, Olivia was aware of a deep unease. Her godmother seemed to be suggesting that Ellen's marriage had been a mistake – that she had made the wrong choice between two friends. Why, she wondered, had Jack Fratton been the wrong man, in Alice's opinion? Her mother had obviously been in love with him and not the other man because they were engaged . . . and why was her godmother so determinedly short on details and explanations? She was hinting at a mystery surrounding Ellen's marriage but without revealing her reasons for doing so and Olivia was beginning to feel annoyed. The four Fratton 'children' were all adults now and surely deserved the full truth instead of a trickle of information designed to make them more confused about their father's return.

'And you are no longer planning to come to the wedding!' she accused the absent Alice. 'Is this really because you are desperately busy or because you don't wish to meet Father?' Her shoulders sagged as she realized how disappointed Isabel would be if her godmother failed to attend the wedding. 'And *I* shall be the one who has to break the bad news!' she muttered.

Refolding the letter she resolved to show it to Theo at the

first opportunity but that would do nothing to prevent her father suddenly appearing on their doorstep. Did he intend to take them by surprise or would he have the decency to give them prior notice of his arrival?

Four

Isabel came into the garden an hour later to find her sister weeding half-heartedly in an effort to tidy the garden before the day of the wedding.

'Where's Luke?' Isabel demanded as her sister straightened up, one hand at her aching back. 'He's not in the house and his bed hasn't been slept in.'

'Don't ask me! I'm not his keeper.' Olivia kept her tone level but her heart sank. Two nights earlier the same thing had happened and Olivia had assumed that there might be a young woman involved and had hoped that Isabel had been unaware of the fact. The coming wedding was already making Izzie ultra-sensitive. Cicely had already put her sister-in-law's nose out of joint by falling pregnant at what Izzie called 'an inconvenient time' and Olivia did not want Luke to produce a lady friend who would further complicate Isabel's big event by diverting more of the limelight.

'It's a bit odd, isn't it?' Isabel reached idly down, pulled up a dandelion and added it to the small pile of weeds Olivia had amassed.

To change the unwelcome subject, Olivia asked, 'When is Miss Denny due? I'm looking forward to seeing the beadwork.' She glanced at Isabel who seemed surprisingly unimpressed by the prospect.

'He's probably with that woman from the Coach and Horses.' Isabel gave her a sideways glance to see how she would react to the suggestion.

Olivia's mouth fell open with shock. 'Woman from the . . . Which woman? There's only Mrs . . . You don't mean Fenella Anders!'

'Yes.'

'Why should he be with Mrs Anders?'

Isabel shrugged her slim shoulders. 'He's taken a shine to her.

Everyone knows . . . except you! I heard them whispering about it in the Post Office.'

'Mrs Anders? But she's married!' Olivia stared at her speechlessly. 'But . . . but what about . . .?'

'He's away. His aunt's dying – or so he says. He's in Hastings to be with her. His wife's running the pub with the help of the barman.'

Olivia needed to sit down but there was nowhere nearby. 'Luke and Mrs Anders? Oh Izzie! Are you sure?'

Isabel poked at the pile of weeds with the toe of her shoe. 'I thought you'd have heard by now. Our "golden boy" doesn't seem— Oh!' She put a hand to her face which was stinging from the slap Olivia had given her. 'What was that for?' she demanded angrily.

Olivia regretted the slap but too late. She had often told her sister not to call Luke 'the golden boy'. Isabel had always envied her brother the attention he received from Aunt Alice, and in a way Olivia sympathized with her but she had repeatedly pointed out that Luke was not to blame – and nor was their godmother. Luke had been born with artistic talent and Alice, an artist, had naturally supported him.

For a moment the two sisters glared at each other and then Olivia mumbled an apology which Isabel ignored.

Abruptly Olivia covered her face with her hands and there was a long moment while she struggled with her overwrought feelings.

'Olivia! Are you crying? Please don't.'

'I'm not crying,' she lied, hastily brushing at her eyes. 'I'm in a bit of a muddle this morning, that's all,' she admitted shakily. 'There's a letter from Aunt Alice. She's very upset about . . . everything.'

'*She's* upset? What about me?' Isabel demanded, hands on hips. 'It's my wedding that's going to be ruined! Where is this wretched letter? I want to read it.'

'It's on the kitchen table but she's . . . Wait, Izzie! Just let me explain.'

But Isabel had turned and was running back through the garden towards the back door.

Olivia shouted, 'Don't forget Miss Denny!'

Olivia stood there, her heart thumping uncomfortably, and even the perfume from the nearby roses failed to soothe her. Glancing down at the weeds she bent down abruptly, snatched them up and tossed them back on to the rose bed. 'Grow where you like!' she told them. 'Why should I trouble myself?'

She walked slowly back to the kitchen wondering about Isabel's reaction to the letter and worrying about Luke. Luke and Mrs Anders? How could she, Olivia, have been so blind, she asked herself. And how could he have been so stupid? She sighed deeply. She had obviously been so distracted by Isabel's wedding and then their father's imminent return that she had missed any clues there might have been to this new problem. Her younger brother with an older *married* woman! It seemed impossible that the unkind fates were finding something else with which to distress her.

The kitchen was empty and the letter had gone but she could hear Izzie's bed springs and knew that she was tossing restlessly, either in anger or dismay. Olivia rolled her eyes despairingly. What was it Aunt Alice used to say when they were young and overexcited? 'There'll be tears before bedtime!' Olivia's smile was a feeble attempt.

'What next?' she asked – but it was a rhetorical question. She had no desire to know the answer.

By the time Miss Denny arrived Isabel had fought down the wave of anger which had overtaken her when she read Aunt Alice's letter. She had washed her face and tidied her hair and fixed a bright smile especially for the dressmaker, anticipating the first occasion on which she would see the finished dress in all its glory. Half an hour later, still in her bedroom, Isabel allowed Miss Denny to coax the dress, resplendent with the new beads, over her head and ease it down with loving care. Soothed to some extent by the sight of herself in the mirror, Isabel's mood finally softened.

The dressmaker positively glowed with satisfaction. She said, 'I've been waiting for this moment! The final fitting is always so . . . Oh my! You look wonderful! Breathtaking!' She stepped back, her face alight with excitement. 'What do you think, Miss Fratton? Aren't the beads the most wonderful final touch?

They lift the dress from being too plain to being perfect!' She clasped her hands. 'Another happy young bride!' she whispered, offering a hand mirror so that the bride to be could appreciate the total effect.

Carefully Isabel examined her reflection from all angles, awed in spite of herself. Miss Denny was right. The design of the dress flattered her slim build and the dove grey of the silk was soft enough not to overpower her pale complexion.

'Imagine how it will be when your hair is dressed on the day,' Miss Denny suggested. 'I did wonder whether you might want a few beads on the circlet you are planning to wear in your hair.'

'Beads? Oh, but I thought we had agreed that white flowers would be best.'

'But now I can see that a few well-placed beads would add a certain something. Tie in with the decoration on the bodice . . . but it's up to you, naturally.'

Isabel pursed her lips. 'I'll think about it. It's all so difficult here at the moment. Pandemonium reigns, as they say! On top of everything else my brother's − well, never mind about him. My sister's in a bad mood and my father's due to appear but we have no idea when . . .' Her voice shook slightly and Miss Denny rushed to ward off any tears. 'Take a look at the back . . . and from the side,' she urged. 'It fits you like a glove!'

'Let's hope all the worry doesn't make me lose weight!' Taking the mirror she regarded the back view with deep satisfaction then turned back and perched herself carefully on the edge of the bed. 'Would you mind if I ask you something?' she began with a fresh trace of nervousness in her voice. 'It's about Father. I don't like to ask Olivia because she doesn't seem to be looking forward to his return as much as I am . . . In fact nobody seems to want him here which is so sad.'

'Well dear, it is rather unusual, if I may say so, and you can't really blame them.'

'But I *do* blame them. He's our *father* and in a way . . .' She sighed deeply. 'The thing is this. I've been wondering if, when he arrives . . . would it be very odd if I called him Papa? I know it sounds childish and I'm a grown woman but I was never able to call him that. I was never able to call him *anything* because he was never here so we never met. We don't know each other. I mean, he was in California with this awful Larry . . .'

'Larry?'

'Yes. He's the man who first persuaded him to go to California – in search of gold. Not that they found very much but Aunt Alice says they did return with a little gold but then later on, when I was due to be born, this awful man somehow lured Father back there. There was some sort of quarrel because Mother wanted him to stay here with us but . . .' Her voice shook and she faltered, tears pricking at her eyelids. 'I don't expect anyone to understand but if I called him Papa just once it would seem as if I had once had a father . . .'

Realizing what was about to happen, Miss Denny rushed forward with a lace handkerchief. 'Don't cry, dear! Take this. It's the most terrible bad luck to cry while you're wearing your wedding dress!'

'Bad luck?' Isabel struggled with her tears, dabbing at them ineffectually with the delicate handkerchief.

A large tear fell on to the front of the dress and Miss Denny cried 'Oh! Now look what's happened! You will mark the silk!' Snatching back the handkerchief she gave a tentative dab at the small wet mark, her face screwed up with anxiety.

'I'm sorry!' Isabel sniffed loudly. 'You must think me very foolish. I just wanted to pretend that he's coming home from work and I'm rushing to the front door to greet him. Like other little girls. I know he can't swing me round . . . I'm a bit too big for that but . . .' Her attempt at a smile wavered as she brushed tears away with her fingers.

A second tear joined the first and Miss Denny gave a small groan. 'But of course you can call him Papa!' she cried desperately. 'Why ever not? I'm sure he would appreciate it.'

'The others will think I'm being silly but . . .'

'Ah but your father may be touched by the gesture. Such a kind thought. Yes! He will understand. For all you know, he may be thinking along the same lines. Oh do cheer up, Miss Fratton!'

'You think so?' She blinked furiously. 'About appreciating the thought?'

'Most certainly. I mean . . . such a sweet welcome and . . . and a sort of forgiveness for all the lost years! He must be feeling extremely guilty. Now stand up, dear.' She reached for Isabel's hands and gently urged her into a standing position. 'We mustn't spoil your beautiful dress!'

Obediently Isabel allowed the dressmaker to blot the damp spots, smooth out the back of the dress and rearrange the folds to her satisfaction.

'I think, Miss Fratton, if we're very lucky the tears may not leave any marks.' She stepped back. 'Or if they do, we might hide them with a necklace. I have something that would look very nice and you are welcome to borrow it. You know what they say brides should wear? "Something borrowed, something blue." Surely your mother . . . Oh! Sorry, I quite forgot.'

'But I haven't got anything blue!'

'Some brides wear a garter made of blue lace – or carry a blue-edged handkerchief. Have a little think about it, dear. I could make a garter for you very easily.' She walked slowly round Isabel, nodding and making approving noises. 'Do you want to call your sister up to see it?'

Isabel hesitated. 'Maybe not today,' she said. 'She's sure to ask why I've been crying and I can't explain. She wouldn't understand. I don't think she has ever forgiven him for what he did to us – especially what he did to Mother – and she's also worried because she'll be left here alone with him when I'm married and Luke's moved down to Cornwall. She seems to think they might not like each other. Luke and Father, I mean.'

'It could be very awkward for her.' Miss Denny helped her off with the dress, put it on the padded hanger and covered it reverently with the layer of protective white muslin. 'Next time I come we'll have a full rehearsal – with the shoes and the little circlet of silk flowers I'm making and you can hold your little white bible.' She sighed happily, her spirits restored by this comforting image.

When at last the dressmaker had gone, Isabel sat on the end of the bed, cheered by Miss Denny's words about her father. Her eyes shone at the picture they would make. 'I might even throw my arms around him and give him a kiss!'

★   ★   ★

When Bertie returned home after work that evening he was aware as soon as he opened the front door that there was something wrong. His parents were sitting side by side on the sofa which was almost unheard of. Usually his father was pottering in the garden and his mother was in the kitchen preparing the evening meal.

He stood in the doorway and looked nervously from one to the other. His mother and father faced him with identical smiles pasted on to their faces and neither of them could hide their obvious anxiety.

'Oh there you are, Bertie!' his mother said brightly. 'Do sit down, dear.' She glanced at her husband.

A sort of prompt, Bertie thought, his heart already sinking.

His father cleared his throat. 'We just want a quick chat . . . before your mother serves up dinner. She managed to get hold of some very nice chops.'

'Wesley!' She nudged him.

'Oh yes. Sorry dear.'

An awkward silence fell.

Bertie looked from one to the other and said, 'What's going on? Why the reception committee?'

His father said, 'Sit down, son,' and pointed to a chair opposite the sofa. 'Your mother thinks . . .' She nudged him again. 'That is *we* think . . . Do sit *down!*'

With an exaggerated sigh Bertie obliged. 'I've had a long day,' he told them, hoping to head off whatever they were going to say.

His mother snapped, 'Just lately every day seems long, thanks to a certain person!'

Bertie said, 'Oh dear! What have you done, Father?' deliberately misunderstanding. He had been anticipating some kind of protest from his parents.

Wesley said, 'Me? I've done nothing!'

Dorcas said, 'We're wondering about you and Isabel – aren't we, Wesley.'

He nodded.

Bertie frowned. 'Wondering what exactly?'

Wesley scratched the side of his nose and looked at Dorcas. Tutting at his frailty she plunged in. 'About you and Isabel

and . . . and if you are sure, in view of this latest development
. . . that is, the somewhat unwelcome visitor, namely the errant
father . . . You know what I'm saying, dear.'

His father rallied. 'We have your best interests at heart, son.
You are our only child. The thing is it seemed a good idea
when you first got together but things have changed and you
have to think of the future.'

Dorcas patted his knee admiringly. 'Very well said, dear.' To
Bertie she said, 'So you do see our point, Bertie.'

'Do I, Mother?' He was frowning. 'Are you worrying about
Mr Fratton? Is that it?'

'Well of *course* we are!' Dorcas blinked. 'And it must be
worrying poor Isabel and it ought to be worrying you. The
thing is it's not too late to change your mind. The invitations have gone out but it's not too late to cancel the
wedding or just to delay it until we know him better.
Naturally Isabel must be consulted before we take any firm
steps . . . Has it occurred to you that Isabel might be having
serious doubts?'

'Not that I've noticed.' He felt slightly baffled. 'Isabel's thrilled
by the prospect of meeting her father after all this time!' This
statement was met by blank stares.

His mother said, 'Thrilled? Oh no, dear! I'm sure she is
making the best of a bad job but she needs help to sort out
her true feelings and she has no one to turn to except us.'

Bertie shrugged. 'I can assure you both there is nothing to
worry about. Absolutely nothing.'

'Really? Nothing at all?' Her tone was wistful.

Bertie shook his head. 'Izzie has hinted that if they know
in advance when he's due they might delay the wedding
because she wants him to walk her down the aisle but apart
from that . . .'

Wesley said, 'Walk her down the aisle? Good Lord! I thought
Theo was—'

Dorcas had brightened a little. 'Delay it? Oh, do you think
so?'

Puzzled, he glanced at her. 'A few weeks wouldn't matter
much if it makes Izzie happy.'

His mother said, 'You're not worried, then, about what sort

of man he is? I mean we know nothing about him except that he walked out on his family and never came back!'

'He must have had his reasons but what difference does it make now? Lord's sake! Izzie is marrying *me*, not her father!'

Wesley bristled. 'That's no way to speak to your mother, Bertie!'

Dorcas said, 'How could she marry him? He's her father!'

Bertie groaned. 'Exactly. That was just a figure of speech. Please listen to me, both of you. Izzie and I are in love with each other and nothing will change that. Her father could be . . . the Pope for all I care. Or an axe murderer!'

'Bertie!' Dorcas cried, one hand to her heart. 'Don't say such terrible things! The Pope! Really!'

Bertie stood up, grinning. 'It was a joke, Mother! Forget I said it.' He looked at his father. 'Nothing and no one is going to come between Izzie and me so do stop worrying.' He stood up and his grin broadened. 'Actually I've got a bit of news of my own. I heard on the grapevine that my senior colleague is going to be promoted at the beginning of next year – to floor manager – and—'

'Oh Bertie! That's not fair. I thought—'

'Certainly it's fair, Mother. He's older than me and he's been there longer. But guess who is going to take his place?'

Dorcas gasped. 'Oh Bertie! You don't mean . . . Is it you?'

'The same!'

'*Bertie!*' She looked at her husband, her earlier worries immediately banished from her mind. 'Promotion! Oh Wesley! Bertie is going to be promoted. Isn't that wonderful!'

Wesley stood up and shook his son's hand. 'That's very welcome news, son. A step in the right direction.'

Dorcas stood up and hugged him.

He said, 'Could we eat a little later tonight? Say half an hour? I want to pop over to tell Izzie the good news.'

'Of course, dear! No problem at all. I'll put the potatoes on half an hour later. Her family will be impressed!'

Minutes later they watched him pedal away and for a long moment neither spoke.

Then Wesley said, 'I dare say when all's said and done, we

shall have to leave it up to them. We've done our duty. We've warned him. We can't do more than that. We've given him something to think about. Let's just put it out of our minds.'

'Put it out of our minds? I wish I could . . . but promotion! Just imagine!'

'And as for Isabel, we must accept that our son knows what he wants. He's a grown man, Dorcas.'

'It seems only yesterday he was being made a prefect! But you're right. We'll see how things go.' She giggled. 'Pope indeed!'

Smiling, he said, 'That's Bertie for you!'

'It is indeed!'

The clock struck one a.m. and Olivia stared up at the dark ceiling feeling more hopeless than usual. More than anything she longed for sleep but there was so much to worry about and now the rain had started in earnest and she knew it might find its way in above the back door and drip on to the mat.

'So get up and go downstairs and move the mat!' she told herself but then the familiar reasons why she should *not* go downstairs filled her mind. She was not responsible for everything that happened. She simply happened to be the eldest family member residing in the house now that Theo had moved out. She organized everything because somebody had to do it but she frequently felt 'put upon'.

'I am not your mother!' she muttered. 'I am just as lost as you are. I am the sad little spinster. Don't expect me to solve all the problems because I can't . . .'

Perhaps she should ask the local handyman to take a look at the door frame. Maybe he could seal the leak with something.

To lessen the sound of the persistent rain, she turned on to her side so that one ear was against the pillow.

'We'll have plenty of problems for you, Father,' she told her absent parent, 'so don't think it will be all wine and roses when you come home!' If he was returning to England to avoid problems in America he would be disappointed to find plenty to worry about here. There was a little rivalry developing between Izzie and Cicely. The first grandchild was due a week before Isabel's wedding. 'Your youngest son, Father, is involved with a married woman . . . and your older daughter is very firmly 'on the shelf' and may end up as an embittered old maid!' There was also money needed to do maintenance on the house and to top it all, Olivia had not been invited by Izzie to see her finished wedding dress.

'A bad sign!' she said with a sigh. 'I'm out of favour.'

Restlessly she turned over on to the other side and closed her eyes. 'Sleep!' she said firmly.

Minutes later she was thinking about Luke and Fenella Anders. During the afternoon she had scoured her mind for anything she knew about the woman. Fenella was a pleasant-looking woman, probably about thirty and with no children. Her husband Will was presently away and maybe Fenella was lonely. Luke was a good-looking young man and it would be easy to see how a casual friendship might have turned into something deeper. The trouble was the news would spread like a wild fire in heather and before long Will Anders would hear the rumours that his wife was being unfaithful.

And what on earth would happen when he did? Olivia was reluctant to say anything to Luke.

Firstly, as she reminded herself, it was not her business, scarcely older than he was and with no more understanding of the world and how it wags.

Secondly, if she were honest, a tiny part of her did not want to spoil things for her brother. No doubt he was deeply in love for the first time – or fancied he was – and she envied him those emotions with all her heart. She had no strong wish to be the one to snatch away his happiness. Soon enough he would be called away by Aunt Alice to 'pay court' to her in Cornwall and no doubt that would be the end of the affair – if it was anything as serious as an affair. She did not envy him his 'wonderful future'! Aunt Alice had very strong beliefs and was not afraid to voice them and during her spell as surrogate mother to the Fratton children she had been kindly but very firm. She liked to get her own way and woe betide those who failed to conform.

Olivia had often wondered how different their upbringing would have been if Ellen had lived. It was not that she did not understand how lucky they were to have an Aunt Alice – the alternative of an orphanage was too dreadful to imagine although, as a young girl, Olivia had often tried. It was simply that the idea of a 'normal' family life with mother and father had always sounded ideal.

Thirdly, she did not know what to say to Luke about his relationship with Fenella Anders. Would Jack Fratton know how to deal with it? What experience did her father have of understanding a son recently grown to manhood? None at all, she reminded herself bitterly, because he had relinquished the role of wise parent when Luke was only a two year old. Unless, she told herself, one of his revelations would be another relationship and possibly more children.

'And when exactly are you planning to arrive, Father?' she said softly. 'Will you turn up at the wedding like a ghost from the past?' She tried to visualize a weather-beaten man with a large hat and a knapsack on his back, making his way slowly down the aisle in the middle of the service. Whatever would the wedding guests make of him?

Or maybe there would be a loud knock at their door in the middle of the night . . . or he might turn up in the middle of the day, having drunk too much by way of fortifying himself for the ordeal. She frowned. She had been thinking about the effect he might have on their lives but now she wondered what effect they would have on him. Now that the time was near, he might be terrified by the prospect of a hostile welcome.

'It would serve you right!' she told him.

Receiving no answer to her earlier question about the date of her father's arrival, Olivia gave up. All she wanted was a few hours of oblivion, she told herself. Was that too much to ask? Turning on to her back she closed her eyes, just as the church bells sounded the first quarter after one.

Five

Olivia was in the garden three days later, pegging up a few items of washing, when Dorcas Hatterly appeared round the side of the house, complaining that no one had answered her knock on the front door.

'I wondered if you would be in the garden,' she explained. 'I do hope you don't mind. I thought we should have a little talk — if you can spare the time.'

'By all means. Come inside and I'll make a pot of tea.' She smiled to hide her nervousness. What was this about, she wondered.

As soon as they were settled in the front room, Mrs Hatterly stirred her tea but made no attempt to drink it. 'It's about the wedding breakfast,' she began. 'As you know my husband is insisting that we pay for everything as our wedding present to the happy couple — wine, beer and all the food but of course we have no firm idea how many people will be attending the wedding.' She opened her purse and produced a folded sheet of paper. 'We had ten names when we sent out our invitations — that includes my parents and my husband's mother — his father is dead. An aunt and uncle, Bertie's godfather, a school friend of mine who adores Bertie as if he were her own son — if she had a son, that is — and her daughter . . . and the two of us. We're not sure how many were sent out on your side or if there have been any late additions.'

'I don't think—'

'Your father, for instance. Money is no object, of course, but we must make quite sure there is enough.'

Olivia tried to hide her dismay. 'That sounds very reasonable,' she stammered. 'Izzie made up her own list but I didn't see it. As you probably know we have a very small family. My father's family have never kept in touch and my mother's parents died within a few years of her death.' She frowned. 'I always wondered whether they died of shock or grief.'

'A little of both, maybe. It must have been a terrible time for you. Thank heavens for your Aunt Alice.' She brightened. 'We are very much looking forward to meeting her, naturally.'

'Yes indeed . . . except that she runs an art gallery and they are having a major exhibition very soon and she may not be able to be here. The mayor is going to be present, apparently, and she is very pleased about that but dare not be absent on the great day!'

'The mayor! How wonderful. I shall tell Wesley. He'll be very pleased.'

She looked genuinely impressed, thought Olivia and added, 'But unfortunately she is also very elderly and not always well enough to travel.' Did that sound reasonable, she wondered.

'And your father? Will he be with us?' Her tone was determinedly casual but Olivia realized that this question was actually the point of her visit.

Olivia decided to be as frank as possible. 'We don't know when he will reach England,' she said. 'Simply that he is on his way back to this country. He might be already in the country but we have no way of telling. As you can imagine it has been something of a shock.'

'After all these years? I should think it is!' Her smile was a little strained. 'Izzie is obviously very excited about meeting him. We wonder if perhaps his return has . . . how shall I put it? His return may have distracted her a little from the wedding.' She made no effort to hide the reproach.

Recognizing the danger signs, Olivia said quickly, 'Nothing could distract my sister from her wedding, Mrs Hatterly. I can set your minds at rest on that point. Only a day or two ago the dressmaker was here for the final fitting. Izzie talks about nothing else. But I won't pretend it is an easy situation and we are all doing our best to stay calm and deal with it.'

Mrs Hatterly nodded. 'Then you don't think she will want to delay the wedding until he can be present – only I'm afraid we may have to change the date of the wedding and that means notifying the guests and altering the date for the caterers.'

'Barring illness, you can rest assured we have no plans to change the date – and we have booked a photographer.'

Belatedly Mrs Hatterly sipped her tea. 'Our only child leaving home! We shall miss Bertie dreadfully but they have found a charming flat. Somewhat on the small side but quite sufficient for now. You must insist on seeing it. Of course it's furnished but there are still things that they can add of their own. I am giving them my second best china which was passed on to me by an elderly aunt some five years ago.'

'I'm sure they are delighted.'

'And we have sorted out some rather nice linen for the table with matching serviettes – we have always had more than we needed – but I have to confess they are difficult to iron and probably not for everyday use. Oh! And a patchwork quilt which I made years ago but which is still in very good condition and Izzie was very "taken" with it when I showed it to her.'

Olivia wondered belatedly if the Frattons had anything worth passing on to the engaged couple. 'Unfortunately most of our furniture belongs to Aunt Alice and came with the house, so to speak, but I'm sure she would be very generous if Bertie and Izzie need anything specific.' She searched her mind for anything else. 'And Mrs Whinnie along the road has offered them an umbrella stand although their hallway is rather narrow . . . and Luke and I have bought them a carriage clock for their mantel-piece although they haven't seen it yet. It's wrapped up on top of the wardrobe.' It all sounded rather tame by comparison, she thought, but all contributions should be gratefully received.

Fifteen minutes later, as Olivia walked with her visitor to the front gate, the thought grew that Izzie *had* had been very diffident about showing off the flat that would be their first home. Surely it should have been a great excitement. Maybe she *was* becoming distracted from the wedding and more concerned with her father's return. Olivia was aware of a frisson of apprehension as she gathered up the teacups and turned back towards the kitchen. Everyone was feeling nervous, she thought, and with good reason. A few imponderables were creeping in. Maybe Jack Fratton was going to be the straw that broke the camel's back!

She quickened her steps. Today was one of her 'reading days' and Mrs Whinnie would be expecting her in less than ten minutes.

★   ★   ★

Mrs Whinnie was a wealthy widow, eighty years old and suffering from poor eyesight and acute rheumatism. The latter meant that she was fairly immobile and spent most of her time alone – apart from a daily live-in maid – and frequently bored. When they had first met Olivia had offered, out of the kindness of her heart, to read to her once a week, but instead of accepting, Mrs Whinnie had insisted that instead they made it two days a week for an hour, to be paid for at a very fair rate which Olivia could not refuse.

Mrs Whinnie's home, about sixty yards further down the road, was a superior building to Laurel House, having an extra bedroom, a larger garden and being in a better condition.

'So Miss Fratton,' she began as soon as Olivia had settled herself on the seat opposite, 'What is this I hear about your father? Rather a late appearance, I would say, wouldn't you? After how many years?'

Groaning inwardly, Olivia forced a smile. 'Twenty years.'

'Hm! Quite a shock for you, I suspect.' She regarded Olivia thoughtfully, her lips pursed in disapproval. Her hair was piled elaborately on top of her head and held in place with the sort of lace cap favoured by Queen Victoria. She had once been a beauty and had been married three times to rich men who had left her well provided for. She gave Olivia a penetrating stare. 'Will he be welcomed after all this time? After years of neglect?'

Olivia's smile faded. These questions, she realized, were going to become more common once the news spread. She understood people's interest but how could she answer, even if she wanted to? She had no idea how she would feel towards Jack Fratton. Ignoring the question she opened the *Ladies Journal* which waited as usual on a small table, and began to turn the pages.

'Olivia?' Mrs Whinnie had no intention of being denied an answer.

'We shall see,' Olivia told her reluctantly. 'I'm reserving judgement until we meet. That seems the sensible thing to do.'

'Hmm.' Mrs Whinnie reached forward and rang a small brass bell. When the maid entered the room she said, 'A tray of tea and biscuits, please. And have you swept the landing – and the top stairs?'

'Yes, Mrs Whinnie – all except the top stairs but I remembered to iron your nightdress.'

'Good girl.' As soon as the girl had left the room Mrs Whinnie rolled her eyes. 'Millie's very willing but has a head full of sawdust. Can't remember things. Needs constant prompting.'

Seizing her opportunity to keep the conversation away from Jack Fratton's return, Olivia began to read the second episode of a serial in the magazine which Mrs Whinnie had been enjoying. Adopting a slightly tragic tone of voice she began. '*Veronica sighed deeply and her blue eyes darkened with the pain of remembering. The sense of loss—*'

Mrs Whinnie snorted. 'We all suffer loss at some time in our lives. Veronica should pull herself together. What was I saying?'

'*—hung over her like a dark shroud of misery and she covered her face with her hands, pressing her slim fingers—*'

'Oh yes! About your father. There were a lot of rumours at the time, you know. People will always talk – I blame the servants. They know too much and they gossip at every opportunity. I suspect it is bred into them!' She smiled thinly. 'Have you ever noticed nannies in the park? They seat on the seats and gossip to other nannies. You can tell them a thousand times but they will talk. My sister had several nannies and she despaired of them.' She shrugged. 'Maybe it's a universal failing. I dare say most people like to talk.'

You obviously do, thought Olivia, but then so do I if I'm honest. Crossing her fingers she hoped Mrs Whinnie would elaborate on the rumours she had mentioned.

'People like me,' Mrs Whinnie continued, 'who have no one in the world and nothing else to think about!'

Olivia felt obliged to protest. 'I wouldn't say that.'

'Of course you would. Anyway, let's just say it was common knowledge that he'd deserted your mother – just slipped away in the night without even a goodbye to a wife who was expecting another child.' She looked at Olivia expectantly as though challenging Olivia to deny it or defend him.

Doggedly Olivia continued the saga. '*—pressing her fingers against closed eyes to hide her growing despair—*' Olivia was forced to snatch a breath and Mrs Whinnie pounced.

'Naturally people thought there must be another woman but then they were all saying that he'd gone back to California to be with his friend. Lawrence Something-beginning-with-K. Or maybe it was Leonard.' She shrugged again. 'But really! America of all places! Now, my argument was that if America was so wonderful why didn't he take the family with him?' She was stopped by the appearance of the maid with the tray.

Olivia, her thoughts in a whirl at this unexpected outburst, nodded her thanks to the maid and smiled but could say nothing. Part of her wanted to jump to her feet and rush from the house but another part wanted to know more.

Mrs Whinnie said, 'Don't just stand there, girl. Put the tray on the table. That's better. Now, did you water the geraniums in the garden room?' Her eyes narrowed as the girl shook her head. 'As I thought! Do it at once – after you've done the top stairs!'

At that moment Mrs Whinnie's Pekinese dog trotted into the room and looked up at her mistress with longing but she said,' You can see I'm busy, Sukey. You'll have to wait.'

The girl hurried from the room and Mrs Whinnie started to pour the tea. 'Help yourself to a biscuit,' she told Olivia.

Reluctantly Olivia obeyed. 'I'm sure Father was doing what he thought best,' she said but it sounded unconvincing. She did not believe it herself but felt under some obscure obligation to defend him.

'Nonsense!'

The dog began to whine then gave a small bark. Mrs Whinnie tutted. 'What did I say, Sukey? I know you want to come on my lap but I've said no. No means no, so do stop fussing.'

She stared at the selection of biscuits. 'The chocolate finger has gone,' she remarked. 'It always does. I think the girl helps herself . . . Now where was I? Oh yes. That friend of his was a bad influence. Word has it that he encouraged your father to defect from his duties to the family. Oh yes! A weak man like your father can easily be influenced.'

Olivia said stiffly, 'I'm sure my father was not a weak man. He was—'

'Not weak? Good heavens, Miss Fratton! Face facts.'

Sukey fidgeted, and began to whimper for attention. Mrs Whinnie glared at the animal. 'Remember your manners, Sukey! You do not interrupt when I'm talking!' She shook her head. 'I sometimes wonder, Olivia, if this silly dog understands English. The breed comes from China, I believe, or is it Japan, so maybe . . .' She shrugged. 'What was I saying? Oh yes, this Leonard fellow was single so he had no responsibilities. That's what I heard. He could wander off to Timbuktu and nobody would be inconvenienced, but your father was different.'

Discouraged, the dog suddenly turned and padded away in the direction of the door. Mrs Whinnie cried, 'Oh! Sukey, darling! Don't go. Did I hurt your feelings then? Really, what a fuss! I simply told you not to interrupt me when I'm talking.'

Sukey scuttled back, her fluffy tail wagging furiously, and Mrs Whinnie reached down and lifted the dog on to her lap. Sukey gave a sigh of pleasure and at once settled down.

Mrs Whinnie resumed her story. 'There was a terrible quarrel earlier that evening, so I heard. Shouting and screaming. It was too far away for *me* to hear anything but the neighbours on either side heard it and it quickly became common know-ledge. There was a woman involved – a friend of the family – and she was shrieking in anger. She was something glamorous, I believe. Rich and glamorous.' She reached carefully over the dog for her teacup. 'Some said she was an actress or a singer . . .' She frowned. 'But she might have been an artist. These arty types can be very temperamental, I believe. Very highly strung. It's the nature of the beast.'

By this time Olivia was too fascinated to protest at this description of Alice and she guiltily said nothing in her godmother's defence. She was wondering how much, if anything, she would repeat of this conversation when she went home. Better maybe to let sleeping dogs lie, she thought – or maybe she would confide in Theo.

'Quite a scandal at the time,' Mrs Whinnie said, straightening her back a little. 'We don't expect that sort of thing in Canterbury. We have the cathedral to live up to.' She stirred her tea and sipped daintily, patting her lips afterwards with a handkerchief. Abruptly losing interest she said sharply, 'Go on, Olivia, with the story.'

Olivia found her place in the magazine and continued reading.

'—*Veronica wanted to crawl away and hide – anywhere where she would not be seen; somewhere far from spying eyes*—'

Mrs Whinnie, exasperated by her tragic heroine, rolled her eyes. 'Oh, for heaven's sake, grow up, Veronica!' she snapped. 'You're not a child.' She reached for a biscuit, broke a piece off and gave it to the dog. 'I don't know who writes this rubbish! Turn over to the cookery column, please, Miss Fratton. It might be more exciting!'

Meanwhile events were taking a new turn not many miles from Mrs Whinnie's parlour.

The Coach and Horses was sited alongside the main road into Canterbury but set back about ten yards from the edge which allowed vehicles to park outside. A large sign, depicting an old stage coach, swung from a pole, creaking mournfully whenever a stray gust of wind caught it. At first sight it looked unchanged from when the man had last seen it, twenty years earlier, and he was torn between reliving the comfort it offered and risking being seen by someone who might recognize him. After some deliberation he crossed his fingers, pushed open the door and stepped inside.

At two thirty on a Tuesday afternoon there were very few customers and he was soon established in a corner where the light was dimmest, with his hat brim pulled down a little to hide part of his face. He was soon sipping the local beer with pleasure – at least that had not changed over the intervening years. As a quiet stranger in the corner seat he attracted little more than a glance from those he guessed to be regulars – those who were greeted by name and whose preferred tipple, usually draught beer, was immediately poured for them by the attractive barmaid.

He saw with relief that she was too young to have been in her present job twenty years ago so there was not the remotest chance that she would recognize him. He had made up his mind that if challenged he would reply to any awkward questions in a way that gave nothing away.

Looking casually around he saw an elderly man slumped on

a chair beneath the window, his moleskin-clad legs thrust out across the sawdust floor, a cheap clay pipe in his mouth. An absence of smoke seemed to suggest that it needed refilling. There was something vaguely familiar about him but that was as far as it went. On the far side of the room three men, obviously friends, chatted about a day they had previously spent together at the races in Folkestone – their talk interrupted from time to time by muted laughter.

He felt a wave of nostalgia as he gazed slowly round, taking in the smoky atmosphere, the smell of dust and stale beer. A fly paper dangled from the ceiling, there was a shove-halfpenny board on the table, and a tabby cat slept on the window sill. He smiled suddenly, spotting the old clock on the wall which still said five past twelve. He was aware of a small glow of relief that the new owners had made very few changes.

The Coach and Horses had been their favourite pub, where Jack and Larry were known and welcomed whenever they thrust their heads round the door – greeted more often than not by a mix of cheers and friendly catcalls. He sighed. It all seemed a lifetime ago.

At the bar a young man leaned across to the barmaid, keeping his head close to hers and his voice low, and it was soon obvious to any casual observer that they were more than barmaid and customer. She smiled a lot, leaning confidingly across the counter towards him, keeping her voice low.

Glancing his way, she raised her voice. 'New to these parts, are you then?'

The owner of the pipe had roused himself to a sitting position and was pulling a pouch of tobacco from the pocket of his coat and peering at it short-sightedly, ignoring the stranger.

'Just passing through.' The man's heart began to hammer, in spite of the careful way he had tried to prepare for a moment like this.

The brief exchange drew the attention of the young man who turned to look at him.

The barmaid said, 'Come far, have you?'

To delay his answer he grabbed the tankard, raised it to his lips and drank. At last he said, 'A fair distance.' He was now wishing he had chosen a different pub but he had been a loyal customer all those years ago and it had seemed possible he might feel able to relax and blend in again. Now he regretted the rash decision, wondering if anyone could hear his heart pounding or sense his anxiety. Years ago strangers were always greeted with suspicion. Now he was the stranger.

The young man was staring at him with unashamed curiosity. He had fair hair and a friendly, open face and a distinct look of Ellen that was unmistakable! Shocked, the man busied himself with another gulp of his beer.

The barmaid said, 'You should visit the cathedral in the town before you move on. It's worth a look. Very famous, our cathedral. People come from overseas to see it. They write about it and some paint pictures of it.' She indicated the young man. 'This gentleman's an artist. He painted that.' She pointed to an oil painting on the wall beside the old man with the pipe.

Grateful for an opportunity to avoid speaking to the young man he crossed the room, passing the old man who had now dropped his tobacco pouch on to the floor and was scrabbling to scrape the spilled contents together.

Standing with his back to the bar he stared at the picture and then at the signature. 'Very good! Yes,' he said hoarsely. 'Excellent.'

'Luke painted it specially for us a couple of years ago.' She smiled. 'When he's famous he's promised us that that picture will be worth a lot of money!'

The young man laughed. 'No harm in hoping!'

She said, 'When we took the place over I wanted to rename this place "The Cathedral" but my husband wasn't keen. Said it was too religious. I said, "But Jesus drank wine, didn't he?"'

'Good point.'

'But seriously, you really should see the cathedral. Inside as well as out.'

The signature was clearly visible. *Lucas Fratton.*

She persisted. 'So what do you think of it?'

'Excellent,' he repeated, afraid to turn back and face them.

Finally losing his nerve, he finished his drink, invented a meeting with someone and made a quick exit. 'You were a fool to come back,' he told himself bitterly. 'It's never going to work out. Lucas Fratton. So that was the youngest boy.

Obviously very talented. Very artistic. Ellen would have been delighted if she had lived to see his success. And he was so much like his mother. Poor Ellen. She had missed so much – never seeing the children grow up.

Almost stumbling, he realized that his eyes were moist, the beginning of tears blurring his vision. With four children to raise, Ellen would have needed her husband's support. And might have had it, had Alice not interfered the way she did. Talk about lighting the touchpaper! She may have been well intentioned but she had had no right to say what she did . . .

Not that poor Ellen would have survived the last baby's birth but at least she would have been spared a great deal of unnecessary grief and worry.

As he plodded on in the direction of the town and his lodgings, he wondered whether or not to buy a bicycle – or maybe even a small motor car. The latter had its appeal but was he staying long enough to make it a sensible purchase? That all depended on the family and he had no idea how they would react. He might be setting off again in the near future. More than likely! 'This is not going to be easy,' he warned himself yet again. 'In fact it's going to be damned nigh impossible! Maybe you should think again!'

The auction room was already filling up as Theo made his way along the two tables that held the first of the items to be auctioned. As the number was read out from the catalogue, he would hold up the appropriate item for a last glimpse for the audience before it went under the hammer.

The prospective bidders sat in rows facing the rostrum on which the auctioneer would shortly take his place. Many were private buyers looking for something to add to their collections but probably a dozen or more were traders who themselves owned antique shops or whose job was to seek out items for their wealthy clients who preferred to stay at home and let someone else do the searching for them.

Theo glanced at the items for sale – glass decanter, seventeenth century; an exquisite miniature by an unknown artist; a set of bone-handled knives; a doll with a head made of wax; a snuff box – probably seventeenth century . . .

Michael Rawley appeared beside him. 'I was thinking last night about the book idea. You told me once you had a lot of Georgian silver in that old house of yours. Maybe each book could specialize in a certain period – sixteenth-century pottery, seventeenth-century glassware – that sort of thing. Narrow each one down a bit.'

'It could work,' Theo replied cautiously because he was beginning to have doubts about the idea. Rawley meant well but Theo felt he was being pressured and that if he failed to succeed with the book idea he would be letting his colleague down. He opened his mouth to make the point as tactfully as he could when he was interrupted by the auctioneer who took his place on the rostrum with a cheery greeting. A hush fell over the room with all eyes focused on him and his 'hammer'. He was what Theo thought of as 'bluff' or maybe 'hearty' with a face full of reddened veins which suggested an enthusiastic use of alcohol.

'Good afternoon, ladies and gentlemen,' he said in his familiar gravelly voice. 'Nice to see so many people here this afternoon – both regulars and new faces. Please have your catalogues to hand – plus pockets full of money – and we'll make a start.' He rearranged a few papers on his lectern and reached for his gavel. 'Item number one is a glass decanter.'

Theo lifted it carefully and held it steady so that the audience could examine it.

The auctioneer continued. 'Seventeenth century, a couple of small chips around the top edge but otherwise in very good condition. A well-fitting lid. No reserve so start the bidding where you will.' He looked round the room expectantly.

Rawley lowered his voice to a discreet whisper. 'How d'you come to have so much silver, if you'll pardon the question?'

'Our godmother, Alice, comes from the very wealthy Redmond family. She and my mother, Ellen, were friends since Mother was their fourteen-year-old housemaid. Alice, who became our godmother, was the only child of the Redmond family and inherited the house, which she hated, and with it her father's collection of antique silver.'

Around them the bidding was rising and then the hammer went down. 'Item number two.' The auctioneer glanced towards

Theo who hastily lifted the next item. 'A very beautiful mini-ature of a young woman by the name of Jessica Leonora West, unfortunately by an unknown artist; otherwise we would today be looking for a much higher valuation . . .'

Rawley continued in a whisper. 'And you are allowed to sell whatever you like?'

Theo kept his voice low. 'Not exactly. Alice likes to keep the house maintained while we are living in it so she regularly suggests that we sell some of the antiques. The money helps us to pay for our food and heating and pays for repairs when necessary.' Lowering his voice, he leaned towards the older man. 'There's always been a suspicion that for some reason she feels responsible for our father leaving home so abruptly, but when I once plucked up courage to ask her about it she very firmly brushed the question aside and has never said a word about it since. It's as though that part of our past never happened!' He shrugged his shoulders.

'I do love a good mystery!' Rawley grinned then pressed a finger to his lips. 'Not a word will pass my lips,' he vowed, rolling his eyes.

The auctioneer was now adopting a petulant tone. 'Now ladies and gentleman, I cannot let this beautiful miniature go below the reserve price. Think about the undoubted quality of what is being offered. I am sure it will realize a profit when it is sold on at the right auction. Or it would make a delightful present for someone dear to you. Dig a little deeper into your pockets . . .'

Rawley changed the subject. 'So how's the wedding going? Your sister, isn't it? Isabel?'

'The invitations have gone out! Can't change her mind now.'

'You hope she won't!'

Theo grinned. 'I don't even want to think such a thing. Poor Olivia swears she will be grey before the great day finally arrives – and I still have to write a speech which Izzie approves of!'

Friday, 11th May (ten past eleven!)

I had a talk with Luke this evening about Fenella Anders, which came up because he told me about a stranger who turned up in the

Coach and Horses earlier today and Luke thinks he had an American accent and did I think it might be Father 'casing the joint' – as he so elegantly put it! He seemed to suggest that the man who might or might not be Father may be closer than we think and spying on us. I pointed out that there must be hundreds of stray Americans wandering around England. I showed him the photo of the two of them as young men and he said it was difficult because the man he saw was much older and has a moustache and a bit of a beard.

He said that the man was interested in Luke's painting of the cathedral but very soon left the pub. Luke then changed the subject and went on to talk about Will Anders who is away for several weeks, supposedly with his father or his aunt or someone who is dying of consumption, but Fenella thinks he is with another woman. And that makes me very nervous! But as Luke reminds me time and again, I am only his sister and have no right to pry or even to offer unwanted advice!

Theo has had a brief note from Aunt Alice telling him to sell the two remaining Georgian candlesticks for us – the tall silver ones from the old study. I shall be sorry to see them go but needs must, I suppose. Theo believes they will fetch a few pounds – maybe as much as ten or eleven! She is so generous with her antiques – we could never thank her enough for keeping us 'afloat', as they say. She always pretends the money has to go on maintenance of her property but she knows we would find it hard to stay here without some financial help.

Big occasion! This afternoon Izzie put on her wedding dress for me and she looks really wonderful. She has stopped complaining that Miss Denny was 'too cheap to be any good' and now admits that the design and the workmanship could not be bettered even if we had paid twice as much. I felt a little choked as I looked at her, slowly twirling to show off the dress. We had roughly pinned up her hair with combs. Hard to believe but soon she will be a married woman. I feel I should be talking to her about the more intimate side of marriage but as she points out I know very little, if anything, being a sad old spinster with no prospects of ever being anything else – although she did not put it quite like that!! Hopefully Izzie's mother-in-law to be might help her.

I am still worrying about Mrs Whinnie's description of a terrible quarrel that happened here just before Father went back to California and I shall write tomorrow to Aunt Alice to ask her if she knows anything about it and can throw some light on the subject. What on earth was happening that was so disgraceful that it was being gossiped about by all the neighbours? It is all something of a mystery and it would be helpful to know the full story of what went on before Father arrives so that we might know how to treat him.

Theo's father-in-law sent up a couple of rabbits for Sunday's lunch. He is very kind. I shall add some bacon, herbs and an onion. Rabbit can be rather tasteless.

The following Sunday, after the service, the vicar stood in the stiff breeze outside his church porch, shaking hands with his parishioners as they made their farewells, claiming as they always did that they had enjoyed both the sermon and the service and mostly wishing him well for the coming week or sending good wishes to his 'good lady wife' and also to his brother, who had been remembered in their prayers and who was, it seemed, seriously ill and not likely to recover from poisoning of the blood after dentistry.

He said, 'Ah! Mrs Westbury . . .' and gave her a broad smile. She was a wealthy widow and very generous. She frequently paid for fresh flowers for the church and always made a special donation at Christmas.

'A nice sermon, vicar. Very topical.' He imagined a glint in her eye as she added, 'We must all be aware of the dangers of temptation,' and watched her nervously as she moved on.

Behind her came a small man in a bowler hat: Mrs Westbury's butler, who was always a source of irritation to the vicar who found him altogether too servile. Why did servants have to think like servants even when they were not 'on duty', he wondered, shaking him firmly by the hand.

The butler said, 'Thank you. Thank you. A good sermon. Plenty to think about, vicar,' and scurried past.

A woman took his place and looked at him admiringly, as many of the female parishioners did. 'The sermon was splendid.'

'I'm glad you think so.' He knew her name but was trying to place her.

'Truly uplifting. It gives me the courage to face our uncertain future with strength of—'

'Uncertain future?' He wondered if he had missed something.

'Our Mr Fratton coming home after all these years and none of us knowing what to expect! What changes will he make? I've been with the family for nigh on ten years and—'

'Ah yes! The prodigal father.' He suddenly remembered her. This was Mrs Bourne, housekeeper to the Fratton family – and the daughter was shortly going to be married. Isadora? No, Isabel. 'I'm sure your services will still be needed, Mrs Bourne . . .' He reached out a hand to the man behind her and she took the none too subtle hint and moved on.

'Mrs Anders!' He had heard rumours but smiled nonetheless.

She said, 'We rarely see you, vicar.'

'My days are so full but I will try.'

'We'll look forward to seeing you.' Her smile dazzled him. 'Our good Lord was not averse to a glass of wine!'

'Er – very true. Yes, thank you. Yes indeed . . .' He thought she could be seriously tempting. 'Ah! Good morning, Mr Timmins, so good to see you up and about again.' He stepped back sharply to avoid the swing of the wooden crutch. Mr Timmins was a hostage to gout but, to his credit, rarely missed the Sunday morning service.

He received a shy nod from the retired teacher by way of answer.

Reluctantly he offered a handshake for the gravedigger in his Sunday best – a miserable old man who muttered something incomprehensible. He was probably complaining about the choice of hymns, the vicar thought resignedly. If 'Abide with Me' was not included in the service, the old fellow felt cheated.

The vicar patted the heads of the three Cobbett children and smiled at the parents, who spoke as one. 'Thank you, vicar.' The mother added, 'Very uplifting.'

Only a few more, he thought.

A small mongrel dog appeared, sniffing around, and the vicar clapped his hands to discourage him as the animal had been known to cock his hind leg against the gravestones in full view of the parishioners. The Cobbett children watched the animal hopefully but were disappointed.

The vicar forced a smile for the younger Miss Fratton who had been hanging back waiting for the rest of the worshippers to leave. 'Aha! Everything all set for the special day?' he asked, expecting an answer in the affirmative.

'I need to talk to you about that,' she told him nervously. 'You said I could come to you if I had any worries. I can't talk to anyone else without upsetting them but . . . but I truly don't know what to do or think or which way to turn.'

His heart sank. The rest of the congregation had by this time drifted away and he had been looking forward to the small sherry that his wife would pour for each of them – their Sunday treat to celebrate another successful sermon. 'We'll go back inside,' he suggested.

Sitting with the vicar in the last two pews Isabel explained that her father was coming home but they did not know when he would arrive. 'The point is that I would love him to be present at my wedding and I'm wondering if I could alter the date if necessary – that is if perhaps we get a letter telling us when he will arrive and we know it will be too late . . .' Her voice trailed off.

The vicar had pursed his lips and now sighed deeply. 'It might be possible,' he said slowly. He felt somewhat aggrieved by the suggestion. No one else would use the date for a wedding – not at such short notice – and that meant a loss of much needed revenue. 'In fact it *would* be possible but you might then have to wait several weeks for your wedding, until we have another vacant date. Would that bother you, Miss Fratton? I mean, have you sent out invitations? You would have to let everyone know, wouldn't you? Quite a palaver, I should imagine.'

Her face had fallen. 'It wouldn't matter to me but . . . I don't expect my fiancé would be very pleased – unless I could make him understand how important it is for me.'

'Mmm.' He raised his eyebrows thoughtfully but said nothing.

'Mind you . . .' She brightened slightly. 'One nice thing has happened. We have at last found a suitable flat – furnished naturally, but the landlord says we can take down his curtains and put up our own which will be fun. Bertie's mother is going to make them for us as soon as we have chosen the material and I fancy something floral for the kitchen and in the front room maybe . . .'

The vicar, not paying any attention to these details, looked at her thoughtfully. 'Now how can I put this? Your fiancé would need to understand exactly why you want to delay the wedding. It might seem to him that you are more concerned for your father than you are for him. At such a vulnerable time in his life – you are both very young – he might begin to doubt that you are entirely certain of your feelings for *him*. Not that that is the case, of course, but it might look that way and perhaps you should not put doubts into his mind.'

Isabel frowned unhappily. 'But of course I am entirely certain. I do love him and I do want us to be married. I just want to walk down the aisle with my arm through my father's arm the way other brides do.' When he didn't answer she added, 'It's not too much to ask of him, is it? He's never done anything else for me in my whole life and I can forgive him for that but there's just this one thing I desperately want him to do and what happens? He says he's coming back to Canterbury but now we don't hear a word from him. I love him dearly but he's so thoughtless!' She swallowed hard.

She's very close to tears, he told himself anxiously. 'You must stay calm, Miss Fratton. Do you have any idea how near he might be?'

'None at all.'

'Could he be here already but maybe afraid to come forward? Cold feet, as they say. From his point of view . . .'

Her eyes blazed suddenly. 'If he's here and too cowardly to make himself known to us then . . . then I don't think very highly of him! Bertie – that is, my fiancé – is already wondering if the whole thing is a hoax! I dare not suggest such a thing to Olivia but . . .' She held up her hands in a gesture of surrender.

'A *hoax*?' Now he was genuinely shocked. 'Perish the thought, Miss Fratton!'

Carried away, she rushed on. 'The truth is we have no idea what sort of person he is – my father, I mean. Mother must have believed in him but over the years his mind may have become distorted by his guilt. If his conscience has troubled him . . . who knows? He might be slightly deranged.' This idea had never entered her head before and now it gave her serious pause for thought.

'Oh dear! Surely not!'

'But it's possible, isn't it?'

Abruptly they both fell silent, both busy with the uncomfortable change in direction which the conversation had taken.

It now occurred to Isabel that he could be a totally unsavoury character. He might drink too much and disgrace her on her wedding day. He might even start 'throwing his weight about' and try to interfere in family matters. Was it possible that she was altogether too trusting and that she might come to regret her father's arrival in Canterbury . . .?

The vicar was first to break the silence. Forcing a cheerful smile he said, 'Poor Miss Fratton. It's a dilemma, isn't it? But we must look on the bright side and put aside all negative thoughts.

'I don't know how I can help you except to say if it is postponed, I promise to fit your wedding into the next available space in the diary, but you really should not delay your decision. Last minute doubts creep in, you see, and I'd hate to see that happen.'

They walked together as far as the gate and Isabel thanked him rather unconvincingly for his advice. He thought she looked a good deal worse after their 'little chat' but he told himself everything would be fine on the day.

As he hurried back towards the vicarage, the dog appeared again, barking and leaping about and scrabbling among the gravestones with undignified and unwarranted enthusiasm. Digging for bones, perhaps, the vicar thought with a slight sense of hysteria. His earlier mood of post-sermon euphoria had been quite ruined by his chat with Miss Fratton and he gave in to temptation and threw a clod of grass at the dog.

It missed.

Six

Next morning when the front door bell rang just before ten, Mrs Bourne tossed the tea towel on to the draining board, smoothed her apron and hurried to answer it. A stranger stood on the doorstep, eyeing her warily. Not rough enough for a tramp, she thought, but what her mother would have called 'hardly out of the top drawer'.

'Yes?' she demanded. He looked like the sort of man who offered to buy valuable old china at a ridiculously low price. Her mouth tightened. She had been caught like that before.

For a moment the man made no answer.

She said firmly, 'We've nothing to sell, if that's what you're after. And before you answer I can tell you there is nobody here but me. Miss Olivia has gone with her sister to choose curtain material and I have no idea how long that will take.'

He hesitated. 'Ah . . . I think they're expecting me. I wrote . . .'

'Expecting you? That's news to me. If it's important you'd better come back later – or I could take a message.'

Again he hesitated, giving her time to study him. He was average height, looked vaguely foreign and distinctly ill at ease. Despite the fact that it was Monday he seemed to be wearing his Sunday best and carried a large canvas bag over one shoulder. He had nice eyes, she thought grudgingly, and there was nothing threatening about him but there was no way she would be sweet-talked into allowing him over the doorstep.

'I'm Jack,' he said. 'Er . . . Jack . . .'

Mrs Bourne's back stiffened. 'I don't care who you are. I have strict orders not to allow strangers into the house especially when Miss Fratton is out. She is most particular. Mr Lucas might be back soon but I can't promise. He's a bit unreliable these days. Do you want to leave a message?'

He glanced up and down the road as though hoping someone would appear to contradict her and when this hope died he said, 'Maybe I could wait somewhere . . . in the summer house, maybe . . . if it's still there?'

Mrs Bourne's eyes narrowed. What did he know about the old summer-house? Had he been snooping around while her back was turned? 'It's not,' she told him. 'They took it down three years ago because of the rot. What do you know about our summer house?'

'I'm Jack,' he repeated. 'Jack Fratton. I used to live here.'

'Jack Fratton?' She gasped, taking a small step backwards. 'You don't mean . . . You're not *the father*? The one who . . .' She couldn't utter the words. Shocked, she realized that she was actually face to face with this terrible man who had abandoned his wife and four children twenty years ago. He did not look like a monster but looks could be deceptive. 'I don't know how you have the cheek—' she began impetuously but then realized abruptly that her employment with the family might soon be a matter for him to decide, and bit back the criticism.

'I'm sorry,' he said helplessly. 'I think I'd better come back later. Maybe this afternoon. They are expecting me at some time. At least I sent a letter . . .' He swallowed, looking thoroughly downcast, and once again glanced up and down the road. 'I'll come back. Maybe tomorrow . . . or maybe never,' he added under his breath so that she almost missed the words.

Mrs Bourne was now in a quandary, having second thoughts about the reception she had given him. Suppose he was welcomed with open arms after she had given him the cold shoulder? What would the family say when they found out that he had been and possibly gone again? They might blame her.

She opened the door a little wider. 'I could bring you a pencil and paper and you could leave a note. Would that help?'

He nodded and she brought him a sheet of paper and an envelope to put it in plus a book to lean the paper on while he attempted to write. The note, she thought, was more like a letter – he had soon covered both sides of the paper in his large untidy scrawl. In silence he reread what he had written and reluctantly she was aware of a growing sympathy for him. She was also recalling something Olivia had said one day about her father coming over from California but she had been very vague and Mrs Bourne had forgotten all about it. Of course, over the years, she had heard the occasional snippet of gossip about that night but she had paid little notice when there seemed no possibility of his return to Kent.

Minutes later she held the envelope in her hand and raised the other hand in a shaky gesture of farewell as he made his way towards the corner of the road and walked out of sight. He didn't once turn back, however, and she was left with a fluttering stomach and the distinct feeling that she could and should have handled things better. It all depended on whether or not they were looking forward to his visit. Were they going to make him welcome or send him away with a flea in his ear?

Staring at the envelope she saw that the letter was sealed and it crossed her mind to steam it open and find out if he had complained about her behaviour but she knew from experience that sometimes an envelope could not be satisfactorily resealed.

Then it would be obvious that she had been snooping! She shuddered, closed the door and took the letter into the parlour and propped it behind the mantelpiece, out of the way of temptation.

'Goodness!' she muttered. 'They'll probably ask me what he was like!'

And what should she say? With her hand on her heart she began to practise how she would describe him. 'Pleasant enough'. Was that fair? Or how about 'Nondescript, really.' Shaking her head she decided that in case he might one day take up his position again as head of the family she must step very carefully.

As soon as Olivia saw Mrs Bourne's face she knew something was wrong. 'What's happened?'

Isabel put her parcel on the table and asked, 'It's not about Bertie, is it?'

'No. It's about your father.' The housekeeper was twisting her hands nervously.

'Father?' Isabel's voice rose. 'What about him?'

Mrs Bourne fixed her eyes on Olivia as she stammered out her news – and excuses. 'He was here but I didn't know who he was and then when I did know I—'

'He was *here?*' Isabel repeated shrilly. 'How? I mean when . . . that is, where is he now?'

Mrs Bourne ignored her. 'I'm sorry, Miss Fratton,' she told Olivia, 'but I didn't know what I was supposed to do because you've always said I should never allow . . .'

Olivia tried to hold down her own excitement. She laid her hand on Mrs Bourne's arm and guided her to a chair. 'Take your time,' she told her. 'Just tell us. Whatever happened – no one is blaming you.'

Isabel cried, 'I'm blaming her. My father came right to our door and she let him go away again. She *sent him away!* Now we might never see him!' She turned to Mrs Bourne who shrank back. 'How could you be so stupid? Oh! I can't believe it. He came and now he's God knows where!'

'Izzie! Your language!' As Olivia heard herself sounding like Aunt Alice she checked further rebuke but it was too late and Izzie rounded on her.

'Don't tell me what I can and can't say!' she snapped, her voice beginning to tremble. 'For the hundredth time, *you are not my mother!* And thank God for that!' She turned back to Mrs Bourne. 'What was he like? What did he say? Did you tell him about my wedding?' Her voice was hoarse. 'Is he coming back?'

Mrs Bourne shook her head but before she could explain further Izzie screamed at her. 'You stupid, useless old woman! You've probably driven him away!'

Tears suddenly poured down her face but as Olivia moved to comfort her, she pushed her away and ran sobbing from the kitchen and up the stairs.

Mrs Bourne, her face pale, said, 'Well! I've never been spoken to like that before!'

'I'm so sorry, Mrs Bourne. She had no right to speak to you like that. I apologize for her outburst. She actually thinks very highly of you – we all do – but you can see how much this wretched man means to her.' She sat down on the opposite side of the table. 'Could you please carry on with whatever you have to tell us?'

Mrs Bourne, still breathing heavily, pointed to the envelope and, as Olivia reached for it, said, 'I told him he should write a note and I took the liberty of fetching paper from the old study.'

Olivia took it down. 'Thank you, Mrs Bourne. You did exactly the right thing. Perhaps you would make a pot of tea. I'm sure we could all do with some. This has come as a shock even though . . .'

While she wondered whether or not to open the envelope, she heard Izzie coming back down the stairs. Was she going out? She put her head round the kitchen door but Izzie was coming into the kitchen so she stepped back.

'I'm sorry, Mrs Bourne,' Izzie said. 'I didn't mean it.' Then she saw the envelope in her sister's hand and her eyes widened. 'What . . .? That's not . . . Is it from him?'

Olivia nodded. 'We'll go into the front room and read it and Mrs Bourne will bring us some tea.'

Settled in the front room Olivia said, 'We must read it although Theo and Luke aren't here because Father might be coming back shortly and we need to be prepared.'

Red-eyed and white-faced, Isabel agreed.

'*Dear family,*' Olivia read out loud. '*I came to see you but no one was home. I shall come back this evening about seven.*'

'He's coming back!' cried Isabel, her expression now ecstatic. 'Father is coming here this very night – just in time for my wedding!' She glanced upward. 'Thank you! Thank you! *Thank you!*'

Olivia hardly knew what to think. In a way she was glad the waiting was over but she was also fearful of this stranger and wondered afresh what might happen in the coming months.

'*Please hear me out. I have no right to take my place again as your father but—*'

'Oh but he does!' cried Isabel. She looked desperately at Olivia. 'We must give him a chance, mustn't we? We can't just turn him away. Couldn't we say he is welcome to stay for a few weeks . . . at least?' Seeing that her sister hesitated she said, 'Well, a few days then. We might like him.'

'We have to talk to Theo and Luke before we make any decisions,' Olivia reminded her. 'And remember, you three will all be gone soon and I shall be the one that has to live with him.' She returned to the note.

'*I found some half-decent lodgings and if not welcome will remain there for a week or two and then return to California. I look forward to meeting you all. Father.*'

A stubborn expression settled over Isabel's face. 'We can't let him go back to California. We *can't!*' She fixed her sister with a steely look. 'He has to stay here and . . . and see his first grandchild and . . . and be happy here again. We'll also find out why he left so suddenly and stayed away all this time. Even if you don't want him to stay here with you, he could go back to his lodgings.' Her eyes shone suddenly. 'Thank goodness I didn't try to delay the wedding. Now that he's here we can go ahead and Theo can forget about having to make a speech. It was worrying him.'

'We'll tell the others to come here if they can to meet him. You could walk over to the farm and tell Theo and Cicely.'

Isabel frowned. 'Do they *have* to come this evening? Truly, Olivia, it might be too much for him – meeting us all at once. Maybe we should—'

'They don't have to come if they have better things to do,' Olivia answered crisply, 'but they must be given the chance. Theo has to know he is here and so does Luke. If we start hiding things from one another then Father's influence will not be a good one.'

Isabel glared at her. 'You would say that. You always twist things. And why should we bother with Luke? He'd rather be with his lady friend at the Coach and Horses!'

'Isabel!'

'And why must I tell Theo? That means talking to Cicely and she'll be talking non-stop about the baby and her aches and pains.'

'You sound a little jealous!'

'I'm not!'

Olivia smiled. 'Listen to what you're saying, Izzie. You're getting married in two weeks' time and this time next year it might be *you* with the morning sickness and the aching back!'

But Isabel's thoughts were racing ahead. 'Is the spare room bed made up? If not I'll make it up for him.'

'I've done it. Days ago.'

'What are we having for supper tonight? It should be something special.'

'While you're at the farm telling Theo what's happening you can buy a couple of chickens from them and some bacon. I'll make a big chicken casserole for – let me see – the four of us and Cicely . . . and Bertie if he wants to be included.'

'Of course he will.'

Olivia saw with relief that Izzie had calmed down and was thinking sensibly again. No more hysterics, she thought hopefully. There were a few early beetroots in the garden; she would bake them and she might find a few remaining parsnips. She thought fleetingly that if Aunt Alice lived nearer, they could invite her although, on second thoughts, probably better not to do so. Her last letter made it clear that Jack Fratton was not among her favourites. Maybe the reason for that was best forgotten.

Isabel, flushed with excitement and brimming with fresh hope, rushed off on her errands, and Olivia, watching her go, crossed her fingers and uttered a quick prayer.

'Don't let her be disappointed,' she prayed. For herself, she was not raising her hopes.

When seven o'clock came round there was an air of tension in Laurel House that was almost tangible. The meal was virtually ready because Olivia had decided that standing or sitting around would be an awkward way to have a conversation with a complete stranger but that over supper it might be easier and more natural. If there were any awkward silences they could concentrate on the food.

Theo and Cicely would not be joining them as Cicely was feeling uncomfortable and was suddenly worrying about the child coming early. She needed the security of her home at the farm and they had promised to call in some other day – even if Theo had to come alone.

Luke was nowhere to be found and enquiries at the Coach and Horses had not led anywhere. Olivia, Isabel and Bertie would be the only people to greet Jack Fratton.

'It's ten past!' cried Isabel, her tone anguished. 'He's not coming! I know it! I don't think I could bear it if he doesn't come as promised!'

'Be patient!' Olivia told her. 'You'll wear yourself out, counting every minute. He's not going to travel all this way and not see us. He'll come when he comes!'

'He'll come when he comes? Oh! That's very helpful! Just because you don't care about him . . .'

Olivia glanced round in the hope that she could find a job for Isabel. 'Here,' she suggested, 'could you take the water jug into the dining room?'

Isabel heaved a weary sigh. 'We should have bought champagne,' she grumbled.

'He might bring some. It's not up to us, is it?'

'Don't keep calling him "he"! Call him Father.' She picked up the jug and groaned. 'Maybe if we cut a slice of lemon and add it to the water. Or two slices? It would float about and look decorative. What do you think? It would look as if we'd made an effort.'

Olivia let that pass. 'I think we are out of lemons. We used them yesterday when we made pancakes.'

'Ice then? Ice looks nice and it tinkles.'

'You could fetch some from the ice house.'

Isabel hesitated. 'He might come while I'm outside,' she said.

At that moment there was a ring at the front door and they both froze.

They spoke as one. 'He's here!'

Isabel rushed from the kitchen along the hall and threw open the door. She had planned to throw herself into her father's arms but he had stepped well back and was regarding her almost warily. He looked older than expected, wearing an ancient suit under a long duster coat which nearly reached his ankles. He looked odd and somehow dowdy and Isabel fought down her disappointment.

She struggled to recall the welcome words she had planned but they had gone. 'Papa!' she stammered and her throat was so dry that no other words came out.

He said, 'Yes siree!' in a mocking American accent. 'Jack Fratton, in person. Which one are you? Olivia or Annabel?'

'I'm *Isabel*!' Shocked, she fought down the immediate and

deep hurt his words had caused. She was his youngest daughter and he didn't even remember her name? Mortified, she realized that Olivia, who was following slowly, must have heard. She stumbled on desperately. 'You may call me Izzie. Everyone does – in the family, that is. I'm the one you never saw. You had left before I was born . . . and then Mother died.' She felt like crying. Nothing was going the way she had planned. He didn't look thrilled to see her and without at least a smile from him, it seemed unsuitable to throw herself into his arms and cling to him. Instead she held open the door and said. 'You'd better come in.' In retrospect it sounded grudging. 'I'll hang up your coat.'

At last he smiled faintly. 'Am I staying then?' He stepped inside and put down the bag he was carrying. Isabel took the coat from him and hung it up on the hall stand, resisting the impulse to clutch it to her heart. She wanted to say so much to him and yet he was not encouraging any signs of affection.

She said, 'I'm engaged to be married.'

'Married! My! Isn't that something!'

The words lacked conviction, she thought, or was she being too sensitive? The poor man must be very nervous. She searched his face for some sign that he was genuinely interested but he simply nodded with what she took to be approval. Fortunately, at that moment Olivia joined them.

'This is my sister, Olivia,' she said unnecessarily.

Olivia found herself staring into wary brown eyes. Weary eyes, she thought, but his gaze was steady. There was a tension in his manner which disconcerted her and the phrases she had planned for the occasion fled from her mind. She had intended to say, 'Did you forget something?' which had once seemed rather amusing but now felt totally inappropriate – but so, also, did any words of genuine welcome and to her annoyance she found herself tongue-tied. Surely *he* should say something, she thought desperately, but he remained silent. There was no flash of recognition between them and she felt nothing for him which could be considered warmth or a sense of forgiveness. He seems vulnerable, she thought at last. Vulnerable, confused and out of his depth, maybe, but not guilty. Yes. That was it.

She read no hint of contrition in the good-natured features. It took her by surprise.

After a long, uneasy moment Olivia and her father shook hands awkwardly and she finally managed a few words of greeting and added, 'Have you had a good journey?'

'A *long* one,' he amended with a slight smile.

'Would you like to wash or refresh yourself? No doubt you can find your way up to the bathroom.'

'I'll take you up,' Isabel said eagerly, 'You won't recognize the bathroom. The lino is new and we've had a geyser fitted for hot water! Three years ago.'

He declined the offer with a polite shake of his head. 'I'm great, thanks,' He was giving Olivia a long look. 'You are very like Ellen when I first knew her. Very like her – but I expect you know that.'

Isabel said quickly, 'Perhaps *I* take after *you*, Father. Aunt Alice thought—'

'Alice Redmond? Ah yes. Aunt Alice. I imagine she's no longer with us. I seem to remember—'

Olivia said, 'On the contrary, she's very much alive – but do come into the front room. We mustn't keep you standing here.'

As they trailed uncertainly into the best room Jack said, 'Something smells very good.'

'Olivia has cooked chicken,' Isabel told him before Olivia could reply, 'but I can cook too. I do a very good fish pie with cod and shrimps and topped with creamy mashed potato.'

'Sounds great!' At last he gave her a smile. 'I'll look forward to that.'

Olivia said, 'I thought you didn't like fish – because of the bones.' She spoke without thinking and the words sounded almost accusing and she bit her lip as Izzie turned to her.

With a look that spoke volumes, Isabel rushed to his defence.

'Aunt Alice said Father was afraid of bones in case they got stuck in his throat – but people can grow out of things.' She turned to him. 'I expect you've become used to them after all that time in California. I expect they eat lots of fish there.'

'Er, yes. I guess we do at that.'

Isabel gave her sister a triumphant grin and Olivia changed

the subject. 'Izzie's fiancé is a lucky man!' she told her father but then wished the words unsaid. They sounded 'motherly', she thought. The one thing she wanted to avoid.

Unable to wait any longer Isabel said, 'You have come at the right time, Father, because I'm getting married on the twenty-sixth and you will be able to escort me down the aisle! I've been praying that you would be here in time. You will, won't you?'

'Getting married?' He looked surprised.

Hadn't he been listening, Olivia wondered.

'I told you – and don't say I'm too young because I'm not and Aunt Alice says . . .'

He turned to Olivia. 'You say that Alice Redmond is still alive? I had no idea. I reckoned she'd be long gone. I guess I lost track of time.'

Before Olivia could answer, Isabel said, 'She's really old but no one knows her age. She might come to the wedding but—'

'She's coming to the wedding?' He seemed disturbed by the idea.

Apparently unaware, Isabel said, 'You will meet my fiancé shortly. He's coming to supper. His name's Bertram Hatterly but we all call him Bertie so you can, of course. Being family.' Her smile was brighter now.

Her confidence was slowly returning, thought Olivia thankfully. Being called Annabel would have been a nasty jolt.

A large black mark would have been given!

They all sat down and minutes later Bertie arrived and Olivia took the chance to escape to the kitchen leaving them to introductions and talk about the wedding while she considered her own confused feelings.

Was this quiet unimpressive man someone her mother had adored? He was certainly the man with whom she had produced four children. Olivia was surprised and disappointed to feel nothing for him whatsoever. Even his voice provoked no memories. He was simply a stranger. A man called Jack Fratton. What on earth had her mother seen in him, she wondered, and had she still adored him when he left for the second time, breaking her heart, leaving them under what now seemed to be rather chaotic circumstances, if Mrs Whinnie was to be believed?

She decided to write immediately to Aunt Alice and ask her for her version of those traumatic events. Then she would decide whether or not she wished her father to remain in the house. Unless, of course, she asked Jack Fratton outright to tell them what had happened to split up the family in such a drastic fashion.

She was putting the potatoes on to boil when Luke came in by the back door, his expression carefully non-committal which Olivia usually saw as a bad sign. He stood staring out of the kitchen window, his fingers drumming restlessly on the table. Waiting, she said nothing.

'So no word from the wanderer?' he asked, without much interest.

'He's in the front room!'

Luke's jaw dropped in surprise as he turned. 'What – here? Now?'

'Yes. He's been here about ten minutes.' She almost said, 'And where have you been?' but managed to hold back the words.

Luke considered the news. 'So what's he like?'

She shrugged wordlessly.

'So not quite the return of the gallant and wild adventurer!' Luke rolled his eyes. 'He didn't gallop up on a horse in search of his long-lost family?' He was trying to sound uninterested but Olivia knew he must be, at the very least, curious about their visitor.

'Gallant and wild? Not at all. Rather subdued. If anything I think he probably feels apprehensive. He doesn't know what to expect from us.'

'Serve him right. We don't know what to expect from him! Does Theo know he's here?'

'Yes, but they aren't coming this evening. Cicely's a bit under the weather – whereas Izzie, naturally, is now in seventh heaven.'

He rolled his eyes. 'Bending his ear, as they say! Izzie will probably drive him straight back to California! And what about you?'

'The jury's still out!'

'Hmm. Is that chicken I can smell?'

'Yes. Bertie's coming. He should be here at any moment.'

Luke sat down on a stool to prove how little he cared about their visitor and stuck out his legs. He looked thoughtful and Olivia's heart skipped a beat. She felt that he had more to say – something to tell her which she might not want to hear. The signs were there. Suddenly she didn't want any more surprises so she busied herself, checking the potatoes unnecessarily, and then hurried to join the family, offering to show their father to the room she had allotted for him.

Isabel, however, had other ideas. '*I'll* take father to his room. We've got so much to talk about.'

Looking slightly self-conscious, Jack Fratton followed her from the room taking his bag with him and Olivia found herself alone in the hall staring at the duster coat which hung on the hallstand – a testament to twenty years of life in a different country with different people.

And another family, perhaps? After years pretending that she no longer cared about him or his desertion, she now felt an unexpected frisson of hurt. He had rejected Ellen and his children and they had been forced to accept all that that meant – but had he then compounded the deed by finding another woman and producing other children? Were there other sons and daughters who knew him intimately and had shared the ups and downs of his life in California?

She swallowed, trying to lessen the pain she felt.

'And now you're back!' she said aloud. She imagined Isabel showing him into the spare room. It was not the bedroom he had originally shared with his wife. Would he notice that? Izzie had placed a vase of flowers on the window sill ('to make him feel welcome' she had told Olivia) and earlier, in a flash of resentment, Olivia had been tempted to remove them – to open the window, in fact, and throw the blooms out on to the terrace. Fortunately common sense had prevailed and she had allowed them to remain. Now she muttered, 'Just until the wedding, Jack Fratton, and then you can leave. You're not really wanted here.'

Bertie duly arrived, Luke greeted his father and the supper started. Talk was at first forced as everyone tiptoed around Jack's presence, trying not to say anything controversial. The

past twenty years seemed to be a forbidden subject but Bertie
and Izzie kept the conversation afloat by talking about their
coming wedding.

Luke was unusually quiet and Olivia was worrying about
what it was that was worrying *him*. She was also longing to
ask Jack the crucial question – 'So what made you come back?'

Before this could happen, however, Luke asked a crucial
question of his own. 'Is it all right with everyone if Fenella
Anders moves in with us at the end of next week? Her husband's
coming home and she's leaving him and has nowhere to go.'

Olivia's stomach curled with a mix of shock, fear and amazement but Luke, his chin jutted, was looking at her for an
answer.

Bertie and Isabel exchanged startled glances and Jack, neatly
sidelined, studied the last fragments of his chicken casserole,
his appetite fast disappearing.

Luke went on. 'I thought she could have Theo's room.'

Isabel recovered first. Giving her brother a furious look she
snapped, 'Of course she can't come here! She's a married
woman! Whatever would people think? And we'll be in the
middle of my wedding preparations. It would be quite impossible. You must see that.' She turned to Jack. 'It's out of the
question, isn't it? For heaven's sake!' Her voice was rising. 'We
might have her husband round here demanding that she goes
back to him! I don't want a scandal just before my wedding.
Father, please tell him.'

All eyes were now on Jack who slowly glanced up from his
plate where he had carefully placed his knife and fork together.

'I'm sorry, Izzie, but I'm only a guest here. It's not my decision to make.'

Olivia breathed a sigh of relief. At least he had had the
decency not to take it upon himself to answer. That would
have been intolerable.

Taken aback, Isabel hesitated. 'Then whose decision is it?'

Bertie sprang to her defence. 'Izzie's right. It would be
awfully . . . unsuitable.'

Isabel's face was flushed, her eyes wide. 'Think of the gossip!
It would be unbearable.' She turned to her father. 'It obviously
isn't your decision but you surely have an *opinion*.'

Olivia felt slightly hysterical. This should be interesting, she thought.

They all waited as Jack gave it some thought. 'I think it would be a big distraction for the family at such a sensitive time,' he said carefully. 'Maybe if Mrs Anders understood that, she might make other arrangements.'

Olivia said, 'Doesn't she have a mother she could go to?'

Isabel turned to her brother. 'This is Aunt Alice's house, remember. I shall write and tell her what you are suggesting and I'm sure she will say no!'

Olivia was aware of an unkind frisson of satisfaction that their father could now see what he had been missing – family squabbles. Perhaps now he would change his mind and hurry back to wherever he had come from!

Luke raised his eyebrows. 'Do you think so, Izzie? Aunt Alice didn't want Father to come here but here he is! Just because it's her house it doesn't give her the right to tell us what to do while we're living in it!' They all looked at Jack who did not react. 'Anyway, you can all stop fussing. It was my idea, not hers. She doesn't know anything about it.'

Weak with relief Olivia said, 'Anyway, Luke, you will be moving to Newquay immediately after the wedding. What would Fenella do then?'

'She would come with me if I had my way but she's afraid of Aunt Alice and might go and stay with her aunt in London.'

Olivia looked at him in disbelief. 'So you pretended she had to come here just to upset us! What a mean thing to do.'

'I'm feeling rather mean at the moment.' His voice was flat but Olivia immediately guessed what had happened. He had asked Fenella to live with him somewhere, sometime, and she had refused. In his despair he was punishing anyone and everyone. But before she could think of comforting words Isabel jumped to her feet.

'He did it to upset me! He's just jealous because for once I'm the centre of attention!' She faced her father. 'He's always been Aunt Alice's favourite – the clever talented boy who never puts a foot wrong! Now it's my turn to shine at my wedding he doesn't like it!'

White-faced, Bertie tugged at her sleeve. 'Don't say any

more, dearest. I think I should go home and you might fancy an early night.' He pushed back his chair and stood up – a broad hint that she should do the same. 'Don't let him spoil things for us.'

Olivia knew that this was getting out of hand but didn't know how to end it.

Bertie turned to Luke who had now risen to his feet. 'I don't understand you, Lucas. Do you like upsetting people? Is that it? Do you have to try and spoil our wedding?'

The two men faced each other angrily. Bertie said, 'Don't say another word!'

'I don't take orders—'

'I said, "Don't say another word!"'

Luke lashed out with his fist but Bertie was too quick for him and got in a blow of his own which caught Luke on the side of the chin and caught him off balance. Isabel screamed and Olivia jumped to her feet.

Luke fell awkwardly against the sideboard and gave a cry of pain, struggling back on to his feet nursing his right hand. 'I think I've broken my wrist!' he said, shocked out of his temper.

Olivia stared at him, horrified. His right hand was his painting hand. 'Quick!' She cried. 'Hold it under the cold tap.'

Bertie was now holding Izzie who for once was silent. Bertie shook his head, making no apology. 'It wasn't a hard punch,' he said. 'He just fell awkwardly.'

Jack spoke up at last. 'Hey! Don't blame yourself. The kid was asking for it.'

Luke was flexing the fingers of his right hand and bending his wrist. 'I think it's fine.'

Now tearful, Isabel dabbed at her eyes with Bertie's handkerchief as he led her out of the room. He paused to say, 'Izzie's going up to her room and staying there! I'm going home.'

Shocked, Olivia covered her face with her hands.

Jack said, 'Let it go, Olivia. These things happen. You can't blame yourself.'

Luke glared at him. 'Welcome home, Father!'

★   ★   ★

Monday, 21st May

At last it has happened. Father turned up today and it was far from easy. He obviously felt the strain of a family muddling its way through life, and went to bed early pleading fatigue although I suspect he had had enough of us! I know I had! At Izzie's insistence I had bought a bottle of champagne for Father's first night home but I can see now it was a mistake.

Luke was in one of his difficult moods and upset Izzie, and Bertie punched him and Luke pretended to have a broken wrist! What a nightmare! I was mortified that our 'visitor' was seeing us at our very worst.

Izzie ended up in tears, naturally, and dashed off to bed without saying goodnight to anyone (and leaving me to clear the table and wash up. As always!). Even Bertie had had more than he could bear and went home early. I hate to think what he told his parents.

Father is something of an enigma and I shall write tomorrow to Aunt Alice demanding that she tells us exactly what happened that last evening when he decided to abscond. I feel strongly that now he has reappeared we are entitled to ask the questions that were always discouraged in the past. As a last resort I shall ask Father himself. He is a strange character. I feel he probably means well but no one is making a connection with him, least of all me (although Izzie tries to pretend they are practically soulmates). He has agreed to give her away at the wedding so that should cheer her up when she wakes up and remembers.

I just cannot think of him as 'Father' and prefer to think of him as Jack Fratton or Jack but to his face I try to avoid a name.

I certainly don't want him to stay more than a few weeks at the most and if he won't go when the time is up I shall ask Aunt Alice to send him packing since it is her house.

He didn't appear too pleased when I told him that Aunt Alice was still alive and thriving. I wonder what she will think when she learns about Fenella Anders — if she does. I have dreadful visions of the two of them eloping. Surely he is not going to let Aunt Alice down after all she has done for him to further his career!

Olivia tossed the pencil aside with a groan. The effort of writing when she was tired and depressed was becoming too much for her and she longed for sleep. Maybe tomorrow she would see things more clearly, she told herself, as she put the diary aside. At least the waiting was over and their father *had* arrived although it had not been a glorious reunion.

At some deeper level of consciousness Olivia suspected that something was not quite as it should be but all they could do was await events – and hopefully enlightenment.

Seven

Someone was tapping on his bedroom door. He sat up, frowning, and it took a second or two to remember where he was. After several restless hours he had obviously dozed off without realizing and now glanced at his watch which rested on the bedside table. It was not an expensive watch but it had been given to him when he was twenty-one by his parents and he would never part with it. He had promised himself all those years ago that it would be buried with him. Impulsively he picked it up and pressed it against his lips, closing his eyes against the inevitable pain of loss. And a lifetime of mostly unfulfilled hopes.

With a sigh he slipped out of bed and padded across the bare boards to open the door.

'Father?'

He should have known, he thought with resignation. It would be the baby of the family. Poor Izzie, deeply insecure and now doubly anxious lest anything should interfere with her wedding plans.

'May I come in, please, Father? I have to talk to you without the others.'

He hesitated for a few seconds but then, unwilling to reject her, held the door open as she slipped into the room. She was in her nightdress but wore a dressing gown over it. Her feet were bare.

She said, 'It's after midnight. Does it matter?'

'No, it doesn't . . . take a seat,' he offered, waving towards the only chair. He had thrown his clothes across it earlier but now he moved them on to the bed and sat down next to them.

'I suddenly felt panicky,' she confessed, 'in case I woke up in the morning and found you had gone away again.'

'I wouldn't do such a thing!' he told her. 'Never!'

'Never?' She blinked in surprise. 'But . . . but that is what you *did* do!'

He cursed his stupidity.

'I'm not blaming you,' she told him earnestly, 'although the others do. But I tried to understand and now you are here I need you to explain what happened because I don't want to believe what they say –' she took a deep breath – 'because it makes you sound callous and as if you don't care about us – not even Mother.'

The moonlight was bright enough to reveal the anguish in her face and he sensed this was not Isabel being dramatic. This was Isabel desperately needing reassurance – but what was he to tell her? He searched for something he could say in his defence, something comforting by way of explanation. 'It was complicated,' he said at last, aware that it sounded lame. Poor kid, he thought. She deserved something to restore her faith in her father but how could he ever achieve that? The truth might be worse than never knowing!

Isabel leaned forward, her hands clasped tightly. 'What I mean is – did you love us at all? Especially Mother . . .'

'Oh, Izzie!'

'Aunt Alice said she died of a broken heart although the doctor said it was childbed fever but according to Aunt Alice she collapsed with grief soon after you left and was quite hysterical and they had to put her to bed and fetch the doctor.'

Her tone was accusing but he forced himself not to feel resentment. Alice had had years in which to influence the children against Jack and had obviously done a good job.

Hearing the slight quiver in her voice he felt he had to give her something. 'Yes. I loved you all. It was . . . circumstances. It was so long ago but . . . I've lived with deep regrets ever since. I've tried not to dwell on it but naturally it's haunted me. Sometimes life takes a wrong turn and it's not anyone's fault, and you can never put it right.'

Izzie sighed heavily and pulled the dressing gown closer around her. 'Bertie thinks that some people simply cannot cope with family life and need to be solitary.'

'He's probably right.'

'He knew a boy at his school who was a loner and never had any friends and he's gone away somewhere exotic to become an explorer in the jungle somewhere and he seems happy enough.'

'Bertie's got an old head on young shoulders. He's a very nice young man. I'm looking forward to meeting his parents.' That was a downright lie but it sounded like something she needed to hear.

'But are you going to do it again, do you think?'

'Not if you all want me to stay.' He attempted a smile. 'If you throw me out I'll understand and I'll have to leave. I wouldn't make any trouble.'

He hoped he was easing her anxiety but he was also desperate to change the subject. 'I want to be here to see you marry,' he said. 'Bertie seems a very suitable husband for you, Isabel – and already he is promised promotion. You must be very proud of him.'

'Oh I am!' she cried, her expression changing. 'If you wish, I could take you to our flat,' she offered eagerly, 'which is fully furnished but we are going to save up so that one day we can buy our own furniture and rent an unfurnished flat.'

'It all sounds very exciting, Izzie.' He was keeping his fingers crossed that he had succeeded in distracting her.

'But I'm going to put up new curtains because the landlord says we can and I've started making a rug for the bedroom out of strips of coloured material. Olivia is going to help me, to speed things up.'

'I wish to God Ellen could have been with you all these years!' The words were out before he knew it.

Izzie nodded. 'I think Mother's been looking down on us all these years, helping us in her own way. At least that's what Olivia said and she was told that by the vicar, when we were all much younger.'

He swallowed. 'Olivia reminds me so much of Ellen.'

'Aunt Alice thinks I take after you but I studied that old photograph of you with Larry Kline and I can't see the likeness.' She smiled suddenly. 'What Aunt Alice actually said was that I take after you but she won't hold it against me!'

'She did, did she?' He laughed, sharing the joke but wondering what else Alice had said. Nothing good, presumably. Being jilted many years ago would certainly have affected her view of men generally – with the exception of Lucas who, from what he had heard, could do no wrong. According to Izzie Alice doted on him and spent hundreds of pounds on his blossoming career as an artist. Maybe Alice saw him as the son she would never have. Whatever would Alice say if she found out about Fenella Anders? He frowned. She could be spiteful at times when she was young and she would hardly approve of the relationship.

Abruptly Isabel stood up. 'So you do promise you won't just disappear again before the wedding?'

'I promise. Hand on my heart!'

'And you'll never again call me Annabel?' She smiled.

'Wouldn't dream of it!'

'And you'll tell me if you are going away again? I think you should stay here and live with Olivia because she'll be lonely without us but she's not sure about you because you're still a stranger. But when you've settled in and seem more fatherly . . .' She shrugged. 'What I mean is – if you hadn't gone away, you'd still be here and living in this house and when you grew old we'd expect to be looking after you.'

'I guess so,' he said, his throat tight. 'But I'm not expecting it now . . . in the circumstances. That's not why I'm here.'

'It's not?' She stared at him in surprise. 'Why are you here then? We don't know why you came back.'

'I wanted to make sure that you were all OK. I wanted to reassure myself that none of you were in any trouble . . . I thought if you were not OK I might be able to help in some way. Better late than never, as they say, but I see now it was a dumb idea.' He shrugged. 'You don't need any help. Theo is married . . .'

'And is going to write a book! And might be famous!'

'Yes. You will soon be Mrs Hatterly. Lucas's future is secure and Olivia . . .'

'Do you think Olivia's all right? I mean there are plenty of women who never marry and never have any family and she might not mind. Not that I want her to be a spinster but she is a bit old now. She would be able to live here on her own because Theo and I would be very near.'

'True.'

'And if you stayed she wouldn't *be* on her own and neither would you.'

'We'd have to see what she had to say about that – but I didn't plan to stay long here unless I was needed. I have a life back there . . .'

'Well, I think you are needed here . . . and what about that awful Fenella Anders? What can we do about her?'

He hesitated. 'She's an unknown quantity. I don't have any answers.'

'But can't we get rid of her somehow? Poor Luke is making a terrible mistake.'

He sighed. 'We can't say that. Who knows? Maybe we all have to make our mistakes and then learn to live with them. I certainly did.' For once she was lost for words and he went on. 'I can't put everything right for everyone, Izzie. No one can. It may be this visit has been a waste of time, one way and another.'

Isabel pounced, her eyes wide with anxiety. 'Visit? Is this just a visit? I thought you'd come home for good.'

'Only if the family needs me,' he repeated. 'What I mean is I wanted to set my mind at ease – to rest easy about you. I suddenly had to know. If there's no part for me to play in the family I have a home back there . . . I still have a choice.' Nothing was making any sense to her, he thought, nor to him, for that matter.

She sighed. 'I wish you'd stayed all those years ago.'

'*I* wish I'd stayed. If things had been the way they should have been I'd have stayed. I'm so sorry, Izzie, but I can't explain.'

For a while neither spoke, busy with their own thoughts.

Then Izzie said, 'I keep wondering if Bertie will abandon *me*. I mean, why shouldn't he? The same thing could happen.'

'He won't, Izzie!' he said earnestly. 'It takes one man to know another and Bertie will be rock solid. Men can read other men, you know. I'd bet my last dollar on it!' He hoped he had convinced her.

'But Mother couldn't read you. She must have thought you'd be rock solid.'

'I would have been! That is . . .' He bit his lip, falling silent.

'But you weren't.' Her mood was changing, he noticed, dismayed.

She frowned. 'How can you write your speech about me for the wedding? You don't know me.'

'I'll do my best. I'll talk to Olivia.'

'What does she know about me? She's only my sister.' Abruptly she stood up. 'I must get back to bed.' At the door she paused before opening it. 'Do you think you could kiss me goodnight? Just this once? You could surely kiss your own daughter. It wouldn't be improper or anything. I promise I won't ask you ever again.'

After a heart-stopping moment he said, 'I'm thinking that would be great,' and held out his arms.

After the kiss Isabel clung to him for a long moment before releasing him, and when she finally closed the door behind her he had tears in his eyes.

'God help me!' he whispered. 'What have I done? I don't think I can go through with this.'

Alice, sitting at the desk in her office next morning, glanced out through the open door of her office into the gallery which was busy as usual on a Saturday. A few new faces, she thought – visitors to the town who were killing an hour or so and might weaken and purchase something. People came in to browse and to be seen and to meet friends – a variety of reasons. But if only ten per cent of them succumbed and spent money she would be satisfied.

She turned back to the letter she was writing and her expression darkened. She was at once eager to spell out Jack Fratton's sins on that never-to-be-forgotten occasion but keen to play down her own actions. Olivia had asked for the truth but she would regret it. Alice had said as little as possible over the years, to save her godchildren from painful revelations.

Dear Olivia, This letter will make matters clearer but the knowledge you seek will not make you happier . . .

Miss Shelley, one of her assistants, glanced in. 'I'm sorry to disturb you but we're running out of change.'

Alice rolled her eyes, left her letter and crossed to the small safe.

Miss Shelley said, 'Are you well, Miss Redmond? You look a little tired.'

'I'm never tired! It's all in the mind, Miss Shelley. You'd do well to remember that.'

'Of course. I forgot . . . Well, we've just sold one of Nigel Stott's harbour views.'

'Splendid!' Withdrawing a small cloth bag full of silver coins, she handed it to the young woman. She relocked the safe and put out a hand to steady herself before returning to her desk. 'Close the door behind you, please.'

'Certainly.'

Alice continued her letter, choosing each word carefully in case Olivia took it into her head to show it to Jack. She had no wish for him to argue with any of it or complain of inaccuracies.

> . . . *As you know your mother and I were very close friends although I was considerably older than her. Jack Fratton and Larry Kline were also close friends – it was a four-sided friendship and very satisfying until that wretched gold fever swept America in 1849 and the two men rushed off to try their luck – but without notable success.*
>
> *They soon returned and your mother became engaged to Larry who adored her . . .*

'You were a fool, Ellen!' she told her friend bitterly. 'Foolish, heartless and . . . you broke Larry's heart. And, more to the point, you broke mine! All you had to say was "No". All you had to do was refuse him. You said yourself he was drunk but I suspect you were also. It was no excuse. You could have stopped him!' She threw down the pen and closed her eyes. 'Instead you probably encouraged him.'

She sat wrapped in the familiar resentment until she reluctantly picked up the pen again.

> . . . *Suddenly, for no apparent reason, Ellen broke off the engagement and declared that she was going to marry Jack . . .*

She sat back in her chair and tried to blot out the unhappy memories but after twenty years the pain was still there. Her too frank opinion at the time had almost cost the two women their friendship, especially when the reason for the broken engagement became clearer. Ellen was expecting a child. Jack was the father.

> . . . *Within months it was obvious that your poor mother was carrying Jack Fratton's child . . .*

Alice sat back remembering how the news had devastated them all. Within weeks Larry had left again for California.

> . . . *Although Jack went ahead with a marriage ceremony he obviously envied his friend his freedom. Ellen gave birth to Theo and then to you but the doctor warned that she was not strong enough to bear any more children and that any more children would put her health at risk . . .*

Miss Shelley reappeared saying that Mrs Miller was asking to speak with her and Alice tutted irritably but rose to her feet. Clients were to be humoured, no matter how busy she was. Clients were money and money meant success and her private life must take a back seat whenever necessary. Olivia's demand for the whole truth about the past had ruined her day and had brought on one of her headaches so she was hardly cheerful but must put on a brave face to meet her public.

'Where's her pampered little pooch?' she asked, patting her hair and smoothing the ruffles of her blouse. 'Is that her I can hear?'

Miss Shelley nodded. 'Tied up outside and yapping fit to wake the dead!'

'She has finally understood our rules! We must count our blessings. No dogs. No ice creams. No noisy children.'

'It's taken her a long time.'

Life takes a long time, thought Alice, suddenly weary. The unsettling memories always disturbed her but even before the news about Jack she had been feeling somewhat jaded and unable to enjoy the prospect of Lucas's move to Newquay as much as she had expected. She had been unable to shake off a vague feeling of unease since her nemesis had announced his return to England. Jack Fratton had erupted into her life once again like a long-dormant volcano and he was presumably hoping to live again in Laurel House. Her father would be turning in his grave! That knowledge alone was enough to depress her spirits. Her instinct was to urge Olivia to banish him from the property but that would cause no end of a fuss and at this precise moment Alice did not feel she had the energy to do battle.

Whatever happened in Canterbury, she told herself, it was only a matter of a week or so now to Isabel's wedding and then her darling Lucas would be joining her. She saw her godson's imminent arrival as the new beginning, a new development in her life, the prize she had been promised.

'I've made a success of my life without your help, Jack!' she muttered breathlessly. 'You are not going to spoil it for me!' She pressed a hand to her heart to calm herself and raised herself carefully from the chair.

Taking a deep breath she straightened her back, fixed a smile on her face and swept from the office into the main room of the gallery.

'Ah! My dear Miss Redmond! I hope I haven't disturbed you.' Mrs Miller was holding out her be-ringed hand and Alice clasped it warmly.

'Mrs Miller! You are looking very well!'

She would finish her letter later, Alice told herself as she glanced round her gallery and, as always, waved elegantly to anyone she recognized. Being in her beloved gallery restored her good humour and before long the flutter in her heart went unnoticed.

When the last client had left the gallery and the money had been checked and put away in the safe, Alice said goodnight to Miss Shelley and closed and locked the street door behind her. Sitting down again in her office she read through her unfinished letter and wondered how much to tell Olivia. Too little and she would not be satisfied. Too much and she would be distressed by the information.

Alice picked up her pen and dipped it into the inkwell.

> *But Jack was a selfish man and Ellen was soon pregnant again*
> *and Lucas was born. Your mother became a semi-invalid and I*
> *spent a lot of time with her while begging Jack to spare her further*
> *children . . .*

When the fourth child was on the way Alice had accused him of putting his own selfish desires before his wife's health and now, in her mind's eye, she clearly saw Jack's furious face as he retaliated, calling her a born troublemaker and telling her to get out of the house and stay out!

'But it was my house!' she reminded herself with grim satisfaction. 'He couldn't throw me out.'

Closing her eyes, she waited for a sudden small pain in her chest to pass. Indigestion? The idea was ridiculous. She ate like a bird and there was nothing wrong with her digestion. Never had been. It served her right, though, because she *had* rather gobbled the sandwich lunch Miss Shelley had made for her – thin white bread without the crusts, a slice of pork tongue and a hint of Dijon mustard.

On impulse she now poured herself a small brandy and sipped it thoughtfully, waiting for the discomfort to fade. It took some time however and by then Alice had lost interest in the letter. Having to choose every word with care, in an effort to put a certain slant on the story, was wearing. Being forced to face uncomfortable truths added to her irritation and abruptly she pushed the pen and the unfinished letter into the top drawer of her desk. 'You are not going to ruin my evening, Jack Fratton!' she told him. 'I shall finish it first thing tomorrow.'

Minutes later, she closed the street door behind her, locked it and paused to peer in through the window to see the gallery through the eyes of casual passers by. Ah yes! There was a space on the wall where Nigel Stott's painting had hung. Tomorrow she must find something suitable to replace it. Her face brightened a little. When her godson arrived the two of them would make such choices. As Alice moved away towards her home her mouth twisted at last into a tentative smile. At times like this it was only the thought of Lucas that kept her from despair.

★   ★   ★

The next day Mrs Whinnie sat in her usual chair, fixing Olivia with a steely look. 'I have a suggestion to make,' she said bluntly. 'I won't be offended if you reject my offer but I think you should consider it.'

Olivia closed the magazine she had just opened. An offer? It sounded intriguing so why was she so reluctant to hear it, she wondered.

'I hear that your father has turned up at last. What's he like? How you imagined he would be?'

Taken aback by the old lady's apparent change of direction, Olivia stammered, 'I don't really know yet. We haven't talked much, at least, not in depth but he seems . . . reasonable, I suppose. Isabel appears to like him and he is going to take part in the wedding service and make a fatherly speech.' Although how he will do that is a mystery, she thought, since he knows nothing about any of us.

Mrs Whinnie frowned. 'If you don't want him to stay, will he go willingly or will you have to eject him? Men can be very stubborn. I have learned that the hard way – I was married three times. I know what I'm talking about.'

'Eject him? Good heavens, I hope not. I hope it doesn't come to that.' Olivia had a passing image of herself pushing him across the doorstep and tossing his few belongings after him. She shuddered.

Mrs Whinnie sipped her tea, her gaze unwavering. 'Is it his house?'

'No. It belongs to my godmother.' Olivia could feel her face redden with the beginnings of resentment. Surely Mrs Whinnie had no right to ask all these questions, she told herself. It was none of this woman's business what went on in the Fratton household. She was gathering herself for a sharp protest when Mrs Whinnie spoke again.

'I only ask, Miss Fratton, because I have to tell you that before too long I shall need a *permanent* companion. My rheumatism is getting worse and the doctor has run out of ideas! "Some things just have to be suffered," he told me. Can you believe that? The man's a fraud and I told him so.'

'I'm so sorry.'

'It's not your fault. It's mine for living too long! I shall soon be less mobile than I am already and will become a prisoner in my own home and I dread the idea of one of those starchy nurses!' She shuddered. 'I shall need someone intelligent to talk to when that happens and to give me some support and I would gladly offer you the position, Miss Fratton, if you ever needed to find alternative accommodation. I think we would get on well together and I trust you. We could agree remuneration and you would have your own flat upstairs.'

'How very thoughtful of you.' Olivia was astonished by the offer because she had never expected to live anywhere else but Laurel House. Neither had she expected ever to need to earn a living. The truth was she had never allowed herself to wonder how she would fare when her sisters and brothers had all 'fled the nest'.

Mrs Whinnie watched her closely. 'I would enjoy your company. You are a bright woman and attractive and you should be married by now but personally I don't recommend it except from a financial point of view and wealthy men aren't always available. I was lucky in that respect.' She shrugged. 'But most women do fancy the idea. If you do you should look about you now that your brothers and sisters are settled but you may be unlikely to marry simply because of adverse circumstances, by which I mean your age.'

Olivia was flustered by the rather unhappy role that Mrs Whinnie had imagined for her. She had never seen herself as downtrodden by an unkind fate. For a few moments she searched for the right words.

Slightly disconcerted by the lack of an answer Mrs Whinnie smiled. 'Just say that you will think about it, Miss Fratton. Bear it in mind. I don't expect an immediate answer. You have enough on your plate with a prodigal father to deal with!' Her smile broadened.

Olivia gathered her wits. 'Thank you, Mrs Whinnie. I shall give your offer serious thought.'

'Good. Then please turn to the horoscopes on page thirty. Let's see what nonsense they have invented for the unfortunate Cancerians this month. Last week I was supposed to anticipate a *change in my career*, of all things!' She laughed. 'Since I have never had a career and don't intend to start now it was most unlikely! Let's see if this forecast is any better.'

Deep in thought as she walked home, Olivia was startled to see a small mongrel sitting on the front step and clapped her hands to shoo it away. It took fright initially and fled to the house next door where it sat on their steps, watching her warily.

She let herself in and found that Theo had called in on his way back from the auction rooms, and he and Jack were deep in conversation.

Her brother looked up and smiled. 'I'm explaining the way I have to go about my new project.'

He looks animated, she thought with a mix of surprise and pleasure. Theo had always been the quiet one, always in the background, and she had been astonished when he became engaged, assuming that Cicely had taken the initiative, but pleased nonetheless to see it happen. Two quiet people, she had thought, but now it seemed there were hidden depths to her brother.

'The book,' said Jack. 'Sounds like a great idea.'

Theo nodded eagerly. 'Miss Fawcett says she will give me the name of her publisher so that I can go up to London and talk to him about my idea for a book. If he likes it we might also discuss the format of the book.'

Go up to London? Olivia hid her surprise. She had never imagined her brother as someone who would 'go up to London' – rather as someone who would stay firmly in the country, content with his lot and never venturing further than Canterbury.

'Miss Fawcett thinks it might be a series instead of a one-off. And because I have a good background in antiques through my job the publisher might take more notice of me.'

'I'm so pleased!' Olivia told him. 'Before we know it you'll be a father *and* an author! Good things happen to nice people!'

He grinned. 'I know what you're thinking but Father says if I wish it, he'll come up on the London train with me when I go to the publishers and make sure I don't get myself lost and then after my meeting we can find a restaurant and have lunch together.'

'Better and better!' Olivia felt an unlikely jolt of envy which she quickly brushed aside. If Theo and Jack wanted to go out together, so be it. If she was not included in the outing, she told herself, that was no problem. Jack was obviously trying to be 'fatherly'. Better late than never, she assured herself.

To change the subject she said, 'There was a dog on the doorstep when I came in.'

Theo held up a hand. 'Blame me,' he told her. 'It appeared from nowhere and attached itself to me. Probably a stray. It looks kind of scrawny and it's not wearing a collar. I made the mistake of petting it a bit.'

Olivia smiled. 'I know what you're going to say, Theo, and yes, there are a few scraps of bacon fat I was saving for the birds. They're on the draining board.'

When he'd disappeared in search of them she said, 'Theo always wanted a pet but Aunt Alice was against the idea. She's never liked dogs or cats in the house.' She raised her eyebrows. 'Especially dogs! She hates the way people fuss over them. She always refers to them as 'pampered'! You have been warned.'

'But Theo has a home of his own now,' Jack reminded her, 'and it's on a farm. Most farmers keep a dog or two to keep down the rats.'

Theo found the dog waiting on the step and returned with it scampering beside him. 'I'll give it to him outside in the garden,' he told Olivia, 'and I'll give him some milk.'

When he had gone Jack said, 'Theo is on a roll right now!'

'A roll?'

He grinned. 'Things are going well.'

Olivia stared at him. Their father had gone away an Englishman but had come home an American. Would their mother have liked the change in the man she loved? If she had lived would she ever have found it in her heart to forgive him? Would Ellen think he deserved a second chance? Was there going to be a way back for him? Would living with Jack Fratton be a better choice than becoming Mrs Whinnie's companion?

Without waiting to think what she was saying she asked

suddenly, 'Was it worth it? Leaving us the way you did?' Her voice was hoarse and she felt tears forming – tears which she brushed away with the back of her hand as she forced herself to meet his gaze unflinchingly.

He rested his elbows on his knees and covered his face with his hands. 'It's a long story . . .'

'I don't want to hear your excuses!' she said grimly. 'I just want an answer to the question. I think we're entitled to that much.'

He slowly glanced up at her. 'Without the story, Olivia, you won't understand the answer.'

Abruptly her mood changed and she no longer wanted to hear the answer because it might be more than she could bear.

Instead she sat up. In what she hoped was a brisk no-nonsense voice she said, 'Well, that's that! Now, about your speech for Isabel's wedding – I'd better give you some idea of Isabel's life, otherwise you will have nothing to say and it will be a very short speech.'

Hiding his confusion at this about-turn he nodded.

Olivia took a deep breath. 'With an absent father and a dead mother, Isabel has always craved affection and . . . and admiration . . .'

He frowned. 'I can't say that!'

'I'm not suggesting you do. I'm simply telling you about her life. I thought that was what you wanted. You must say whatever you think suitable on the day.' She kept her tone deliberately cool.

He nodded. Watching her face carefully he waited for her to go on.

'Isabel was a moody little girl – happy and excited one minute and despairing the next. She still is.'

'Did she get along with Alice?'

'I think she wanted to but she knew in her heart that Luke was her godmother's favourite and maybe she didn't want to risk rejection. Aunt Alice tried not to show it but we all knew. Luke was the star . . .' She frowned. 'Alice was never a mother in any sense of the word. She was more of a nanny, maybe a cross between a housekeeper and a nanny. I suppose for Mother's sake she stepped into the gap to prevent us being sent to an orphanage but I don't think she had ever wanted a traditional life – a home, children, grandchildren.'

Even as a child, Olivia had seen through Aunt Alice's attempts at motherhood and had somehow known that her godmother's heart was miles away in a far-flung corner of Cornwall where she planned one day to set up her own gallery. Poor Alice had longed for the glamour and excitement of the art world where she could reign as Queen. How terribly long the years must have seemed, trapped in a mundane world which she had never chosen.

Jack said, 'We seem to be getting a little off track.'

'So we are. Sorry. Yes, Isabel. Where was I?'

He glanced down at his hands, avoiding her gaze. 'I called her Annabel instead of Isabel. It was just a slip. I could have kicked myself. I hope she didn't read too much into it.'

'She will have done but it's too late now.' Olivia frowned then went on. 'Izzie didn't do too well at school but when Alice suggested she go to a boarding school she took it the wrong way and thought she was trying to get rid of her.' She leaned forward. 'This wedding is going to be her big day – the most important in her whole life to date. I'm so afraid something will go wrong at the last moment. She'd be devastated.'

He was looking at her, his expression unreadable but somehow disturbing.

She said 'What is it? Why are you looking at me like that? Tell me!'

He hesitated.

'*Tell me!*'

He spoke reluctantly. 'I don't know if you're strong enough.'

'Probably not, if you want the truth, but you cannot stop now.'

He closed his eyes, searching for words, and while he did so Olivia's thoughts ran riot. He was about to confess a crime, she decided with mounting panic. Anything else would cause him less anguish and whatever it was would make it impossible for her to present him to the family as an acceptable member of their home. Fear was creeping in and suddenly she did not want to hear what he had to confess. She held up her hand in protest. 'No, Father. Please! I've changed my mind. Don't say another word! I don't want to know what you've done. Truly! It's better we don't know. Better you stay a few weeks then just go away again.'

'You don't understand, Olivia. I haven't committed a crime, if that's what you think. It's not—'

She put her hands over her ears. 'Please! I really don't want to hear whatever it is. I can't stand any more shocks. I've enough on my plate already!'

For a long minute he regarded her in silence.

Removing her hands from her ears she rushed on before he could utter another word. 'Isn't it enough that you turn up here out of the blue after all these years, wanting forgiveness?'

'I haven't asked for forgiveness. Not once. Just another chance to . . . Just a chance to see you all and know that you are fine.'

'Then why talk about confessing?'

'You put the words into my mouth. I said nothing about a confession. You jumped to that conclusion. What I want to give you is an explanation of that time . . . the reason for my going and—'

'And not coming back!' She was halfway to the door. 'And then we'll know why you've come back. Is that it?'

'You could say that.' He watched her leave, doubt still written all over her face. Slowly he shook his head. 'You haven't heard the worst of it,' he muttered as she closed the door, 'and maybe you never will.' He waited for her retreating footsteps but after a silence the door opened again. 'Tell me then!' she said. 'The not knowing is worse!'

'Sit down.'

He launched into his account of the fateful night. 'We four had been friends for years and Ellen should have married Larry. It was understood between them. Between all of us. They adored each other. They had just gotten engaged when . . . something happened that was not in the plans. You four children should have been Larry's children. Larry's and Ellen's. You should have been Olivia Kline.'

Olivia frowned, trying to understand what he was saying.

'But then I wouldn't have been me,' she said slowly. 'We would all have been different people! You can't mean that!'

He recognized the confusion in her face. Relentlessly he continued. 'But Larry would never have abandoned you all.'

'So you say!'

'Believe me, I know.'

'You haven't told me what it was that happened although I already know there was a quarrel. Half the street knows it!'

'To make things worse, Alice was in love with Jack – with me, that is. Although she was about ten years older than the rest of us, Alice had flirted with the idea of marriage.'

'To you. That would have been neat.'

He nodded. 'Then one night Ellen and I . . . got a little drunk and . . . you can guess what happened.'

As his meaning dawned. 'You and Mother?' Shocked, Olivia could not bring herself to put his implied intimacy into words.

Jack shrugged. 'Then she found out she was expecting a baby. Theo.'

'So Mother had to marry *you*, then, instead of Larry Kline?'

'That's about it!'

'And Alice never forgave you.'

'And never will. She blamed me and so did Larry and probably your mother did, too. She was making the best of a bad job.' He shrugged helplessly, stood up and walked to the window, his hands thrust deep into his pockets.

'Do you think she ever forgave you?' Olivia asked. 'It was partly her fault as well as yours.'

'Larry never forgave me although we tried to bury the past. Forgive and forget. It's never easy.'

'Larry could have married Alice.'

'They didn't love each other. It was a mess.'

'And did Larry ever forgive Mother?'

'Yes, but it was too late. A child changes everything.'

Stunned by the revelations, Olivia could find nothing else to say and a deep uncomfortable silence fell.

At last she too stood up. 'So that's why Alice won't come to the wedding – because you are here and she hates you – and I can see why.'

'Something like that.' He did not turn. 'If she comes she

will make a scene. I can face anything she wants to throw at me because – I deserve her anger.'

'But she will ruin the wedding.'

He nodded.

'Should we at least prepare the others? They will know anyway if she comes and accuses you.'

'You know them better than I do. Whatever you think best.'

He turned round at last and she saw by his expression how much the telling had cost him. She wanted to feel satisfied that it was his turn to suffer but instead she felt nothing but pity. True he had behaved badly but none of them could have imagined where that single night of drunken passion would lead them. That one false step had ruined all their lives. Ellen married to the wrong man and then abandoned by the husband she had never wanted. Larry Kline, the man who loved her, cast aside and Alice's hopes of marrying Jack gone for ever.

'Do what I think best?' she echoed. 'I don't have the faintest idea!' she told him and left the room on legs that trembled.

Eight

Luke's letter landed on the mat just after seven o'clock the next morning and, by the time Alice had read it, it was twenty past and too early for a small brandy but she poured one anyway, tossing it back in two large gulps and setting the empty tumbler down with a bang – her expression furious, her usually serene face contorted. She was still in her velvet-trimmed dressing gown and matching velvet slippers and her long hair was loose around her shoulders so that she looked at first glance like a younger version of herself.

She stood by the window which overlooked the sea where a stiff breeze was blowing the spray from the waves. She whispered, 'My God, Lucas! You cannot do this to me! You cannot ask this of me! No! Never!'

Fenella Anders! Whoever she was, she was not good enough for Lucas Fratton – not by a mile! There was no way Alice was going to allow her to interfere with the plans she had made for her godson.

'I shall put a stop to this right now!' she declared with false bravado, one hand clutching the letter, the other holding the dressing gown close to her neck in an attempt to stop the shivering which now engulfed her. 'You think you can outdo me, Fenella, but you will find I am more than a match for you!'

'*I am bringing with me the woman I love . . .*' he had written in familiar, delicate handwriting which Alice loved so much. '*I trust you will love her too . . .*'

'Well, I won't love her,' Alice assured him in his absence, 'and when I have finished, you will no longer love her either because I shall show you the money-grubber behind the sweet facade that you find so adorable. You are destined for better things than marriage, my darling Luke.' She poured herself another brandy but this time sipped it thoughtfully.

'The *married* wife of a *publican*! What on earth is he thinking of? Has he lost his wits? Why not a singer in a shabby night club or a . . . a seedy woman of the night?' Sighing, Alice shook her head. 'I lost my first love,' she whispered, 'through no fault of my own. I lost him through his stupid pride. Oh yes! I understood that rash night of so-called love. It was because he was jealous of Larry and mortified because Ellen did not prefer him. He didn't love Ellen and she didn't love him . . .' She swallowed hard. 'But Jack didn't love anyone except himself but he could and would have loved me. It would have come in time. But no! The damned fool had to ruin everything. Now all I have is my precious boy! My precious Luke. I don't intend to see him slip away. Life is not going to deal me *that* card again!'

Abruptly the now familiar pain returned to her chest and she tutted irritably and drew a long, deep breath to calm herself. Damned indigestion! Probably it was the brandy on an empty stomach. She picked up a small handbell from the bedside table and rang it fiercely and non-stop until her housekeeper appeared looking flustered.

'I'll have my breakfast now,' Alice instructed.

'Now? But it's only—'

'Scrambled eggs on smoked salmon, thin bread and butter and a pot of Earl Grey. And then run my bath, please. I have a busy day ahead of me. And pack something suitable for me for at least a three-day stay. I am going up to Canterbury.' To deal with a very serious matter, she thought grimly. Then aloud: 'This Fenella woman will discover she is no match for me and Lucas will fight me at his peril.'

Wednesday, 23rd May, Midday

I think when all this is over and Izzie is safely wed, I shall 'hie me to a nunnery'! It seems that wherever I turn I see a problem lurking in the shadows, waiting to pounce. Jack is worrying me, Izzie is fussing as usual and now Luke tells me he has written to Aunt Alice telling her that he is taking Fenella with him when he goes down to Newquay. She will fly into one of her tempers when she reads the letter but I tell myself Cornwall is a long way away and at least she cannot interfere with the wedding.

To take my mind off all this I went through my wardrobe this morning to find something suitable to wear but only the sprigged jacket and pale green skirt look fresh enough. So maybe I shall buy some greeny feathers and a matching ribbon for my hat and settle for that. I keep telling myself I am not the bride's mother so do not have to stand out in the crowd.

On top of everything else, Theo called in on his way to work. It seems they were all woken in the night by screams from Cicely who thought she was going into labour as she was having painful contractions! After an hour and a half and just before they sent for the midwife, the pains suddenly died away and Mrs Stokes says it was a false alarm and not uncommon as it is easy to get the date wrong so the child might have come earlier than expected – or even later than expected. It all sounds very unreliable.

Theo looked very tired and in need of support but what could I say? I wanted to reassure him but what do I know about childbirth? At times like these I realize how much we miss Mother. Since I could not offer Theo advice I fed him instead – with a fatty bacon sandwich, the way he likes them – and sent him on his way. I hope I didn't make him late for work . . .

Olivia closed the diary and tucked it behind the big milk jug on the dresser. She was immediately assailed by an image of her father, his good-natured face wearing the familiar expression, part hope, part shame; an expression which she now suspected hid something deeper and more disturbing.

He had confided a certain amount of the family's background which explained the hostility between him and Alice but there was still more that he was hiding from her especially about the night of the quarrel – the night when he left home and did not return. Was he going to reveal more, she wondered. She had no idea but . . . did she want to know? Despite her earlier reservations Olivia had been slightly warming towards him but now her senses cried out to be wary of the man until she knew the whole story and that involved the reason for his reappearance.

Had he been in trouble with the law, perhaps? In prison? If so, what crime or crimes had he committed? She couldn't imagine him robbing a bank or killing another man but he might have been a cattle rustler . . . or maybe there was a fight and both men were thrown into jail. It seemed unlikely for he seemed a mild-mannered man, but anything was possible. There were lesser crimes such as fraud or slander or debt, perhaps . . . or cheating at cards. She had a very limited idea of the American justice system but she knew that seriously wicked criminals were forced into 'chain gangs' and driven out to work breaking up rocks.

Staring round the kitchen she realized that she was wasting time. There was always plenty to do and she reproached herself for allowing her thoughts to be hijacked once again by her father. With an effort she went to the cupboard and investigated the contents. No eggs. Ah! She would walk round to the farm and exchange a few words with Mrs Stokes and see how Cicely was bearing up.

While she combed her hair and changed her shoes a new thought occurred. Suppose her father had made a bigamous marriage in America – it would be easy enough to hide the fact of his existing family in England. And then he might have been found out. Would that have earned a prison sentence?

Frustrated, she sighed heavily and whispered, 'I want to like you, Father, and I almost do but I can't allow you to disappoint us all again – that would be more than any of us could deal with. So I'm giving you the benefit of the doubt for the moment but time is running out.'

Two hours after Alice had read Luke's letter she was sitting in a first-class carriage on the train to London where she had booked into the Cumberland Hotel for the night. It was her intention to travel down to Canterbury the following morning and take the household by surprise. That way, she assured herself, the wretched Jack would have no chance to avoid her – and neither would Lucas. If she had signalled her travel plans she had no doubt that Jack would disappear. Anything rather than confront her. In a way she hoped he would.

She also did not want Lucas to escape her by wandering off into the sunset with his wretched Fenella in tow. She had plenty to say to both men. 'Strike while the iron is hot,' she thought. The idea that she might upset Isabel's wedding did not enter her head but if it had she would have ignored it. Alice Redmond had her own concerns and would not permit anyone to interfere with them.

A shilling to the porter had ensured that she sat in a window seat, facing the way the train was moving, with a small table in front of her. A well-dressed woman sat opposite her, clutching a small dog to her chest. The animal wore a striped jacket and looked quite ridiculous in Alice's opinion. For a few minutes she fumed inwardly, incensed by the way the woman murmured to the animal as if it were a baby. Alice imagined a smug expression on the woman's face which also annoyed her but then the woman produced a small biscuit from her pocket and offered it to the dog who sniffed it disdainfully and turned its head away.

The woman smiled at Alice. 'Poor Bobo! He must be hungry but he doesn't like eating on trains. I think the rumble of the wheels upsets his little tummy. He's very sensitive and I fear the journey—'

'He's probably too hot,' Alice interrupted sharply.

'Too hot? I don't think so.' She patted the dog. 'Is Mummy's precious too hot?' She shook her head, answering her own question. 'It's his digestion. The vet says he needs to eat little and often because he has such a delicate stomach.'

Alice's irritation flared suddenly. Fuelled by her adrenalin and the battles awaiting her in Canterbury, she leaned forward.

'May I ask why he needs to wear that coat?' she asked crisply and without any sign that this might be intended as anything but a criticism. 'He's an animal. Surely his own fur is intended to keep him warm.'

The woman stiffened, her smile suddenly replaced by a disapproving look. 'You *may* ask,' she replied, 'but I don't think it is any of your business.'

Alice was accustomed to her views being accepted and she was surprised by the rebuff. She had a few seconds in which to decide how to deal with the situation. She could mutter something which would avert further hostility or she could persevere with her protest. She chose the latter.

'The carriage is warm enough, in my opinion. In my experience animals do not like to be coddled.'

Even as she uttered the words Alice wondered why she was bothering. She had no experience of pets of any kind. The truth was that she needed to release some of the pent-up anger she was carrying towards Jack Fratton and her errant godson.

The woman tilted her head slightly. 'Are you an expert of some kind where animals are concerned? A veterinarian, perhaps? If not I suggest you have said quite enough. Anyone can see that Bobo looks perfectly comfortable in his coat.'

'I thought you said he was hot.'

'No. It was you who suggested he was hot. You blamed his coat which incidentally came from Harrods and was a gift from my sister on his birthday.'

Alice tossed her head derisively. 'Oh, *Harrods* was it? I suppose that makes it all right then!'

By this time the bad-tempered exchange had caught the attention of several other passengers. A gentleman looked on with interest making no attempt to hide his amusement, and two women glanced in her direction and whispered together.

Unfortunately the train attendant chose that moment to enter the carriage and Bobo's owner raised an imperative finger so that, being summoned, he hurried forward.

She said, 'This unpleasant woman is trying to cause a scene.' She waved a hand around her. 'She has been quite insulting and I have plenty of witnesses to prove what I say.'

Alice straightened her back. 'I simply questioned the need for the animal's ridiculous coat. It makes him look like a monkey! All he needs is the organ grinder.'

The attendant's face fell as he realized that tact and diplomacy were going to be needed. Looking at Bobo's owner he said hopefully, 'I'm sure this lady intended no slight. Probably a misunder—'

'Oh but she did!' cried one of the listening women. 'She was quite rude. We all heard her.'

He looked at Alice appealingly. 'I'm sure if you could bring yourself to apologize . . .?'

'Apologize?' Alice tossed her head. 'Certainly not! It's a lot of fuss about nothing.'

Bobo's owner struggled to her feet. 'I've heard quite enough!'

she announced, her voice shrill. 'Please find me another vacant seat, first class, of course. Bobo and I would like to move.'

Alice held her breath. She was herself feeling rather hot and was by now secretly regretting her earlier words and wishing the confrontation at an end. In her present mood, however, she could not back down.

'What nonsense!' she exclaimed. 'I merely made an innocent observation about her dog. I'm afraid she has exaggerated the exchange and is wasting your time but I should be glad if you could accommodate them elsewhere.'

Her pulse, she now realized, was racing with anxiety but she resisted the impulse to put a hand to her heart.

Unsure how to react, the attendant glanced round at the nearest passengers for help.

The gentleman said, 'Really, it was a storm in a teacup. Nothing more.'

As the attendant hesitated hopefully, the second woman spoke up for Bobo's owner. Pointing to Alice she said, 'She was laughing at the dog's coat which came from Harrods. Saying it must be too hot and it had its own fur to keep it warm. She is a very unpleasant woman.'

Cursing inwardly Alice said, 'I was concerned for the dog's welfare. That is all.' Unable to resist any longer, she laid a hand across her pounding heart, adding unwisely, 'Nothing to make a song and dance about!'

Bobo's owner said, 'I'll be the judge of that!'

The attendant took the line of least resistance. 'I'll go and see if there's a vacant seat anywhere,' he offered and withdrew promptly.

Alice sank back against her seat, all the fire gone out of her and matters might have rested there but Bobo's owner sniffed pointedly and muttered something that sounded like 'interfering busybody' and Alice struggled to her feet in sudden fury.

'I'll have you know,' she began shrilly, 'that I thoroughly despise people like you who . . .' Suddenly she felt herself sway and clutched at the table for support. 'People like . . .' she persisted but now the carriage seemed to swim before her eyes and she felt a pain in her chest which left her breathless. 'People . . .' she began again but her whispered words faded as she suddenly pitched forward across the table and lost consciousness.

When she came to she found herself flat on the floor with somebody's coat rolled up as a pillow. The attendant was leaning over her. 'We're just approaching London, madam, and we've arranged for an ambulance to be waiting there. Don't try to talk. No! Don't try to sit up. Just lie back.'

Dazed, Alice tried to look around her. There was no sign of Bobo or his owner but the gentleman who had called the incident 'a storm in a teacup' was sitting beside her. He smiled.

The attendant said, 'This gentleman is a doctor. He's going to wait with you until you are on your way to the hospital. Now you must excuse me but I have other passengers to attend to.'

Alice tried to smile and then she tried to speak but could manage neither. Instead she felt tears of weakness streaming down her face and they were a wonderful release. She gave up the struggle to express herself in words and sobbed silently. The doctor leaned down, took her hand in his and patted it gently.

When she had recovered a little she asked, 'What happened to me? I don't remember.'

'It might have been a very mild heart attack,' he told her, 'or possibly just a faint. You mustn't worry yourself about it. Just look on it as a warning and try to relax more. The hospital doctor will give you some pills and will probably keep you in overnight then advise you to visit your own doctor as soon as possible.'

Alice struggled up on to one elbow. 'It's easy to say don't worry but at my age—' She stopped, feeling breathless.

There was no sign of the two women who had whispered about her – no one except herself and the doctor. She realized she was panting slightly and allowed herself to fall back again with her head resting on the 'pillow'.

On reflection she was pleased she would spend the night in hospital as it would give her a chance to regain her strength before facing Jack again. And there was Luke to deal with also.

She glanced up at the doctor's face and smiled. 'You've been very kind,' she said as the train began to slow down. She would say nothing about this unfortunate occurrence when she arrived in Canterbury. It had never been her way to show weakness of any kind and she was not about to start now.

The hospital staff at St Barts Hospital were as professional as she expected them to be and she was gratified by their care and attention when she was finally installed in the general ward and propped up in bed. A surprisingly young doctor visited her and checked her heart and blood pressure and asked the usual questions before deciding that after a night's rest she would probably be able to complete her journey.

A bowl of soup and two thin slices of bread and butter were brought to her and she devoured them hungrily – pleased to see that her appetite was unimpaired. A sleeping draught worked until just after midnight when she awoke to a dimly lit ward where the surrounding patients snored and groaned and occasionally called weakly for a nurse.

Alice, thirsty, found water in a carafe on her bedside table, poured a little into the glass and sipped it gratefully then settled back on her pillow and pulled the blanket close around her neck, relishing the time to think about Jack Fratton, and as always memories of what might have been crept uninvited into her mind.

'You were a fool, Jack,' she whispered into the darkness. 'I know you loved me. You said you weren't ready to settle down but I knew better. Why on earth you had to seduce Ellen I'll never know! Just to prove a point! That's why. To prove to Larry that you could have either of us! It was vanity, Jack, or maybe simple lust . . . but I think it was mainly vanity. And then poor Ellen was pregnant and there was no going back. You threw me to the winds because you were selfish and vain. Damn you, Jack! I hope you didn't prosper because you didn't deserve to.'

A nurse passed the end of her bed, on her way to a woman who was sobbing loudly. Nurse Allington's shoes squeaked on the polished wooden floor and her starched white apron rustled comfortingly. On her way back to the nurses' station she saw that Alice was awake and in a low voice offered to fetch another sleeping draught.

'Certainly not, thank you. I have a lot to think about and this time is useful to me.'

With a quick smile the nurse hurried back to the other end of the ward and Alice thanked Fate that she had not entered the nursing profession. She had enough to do looking after herself and her career – expending all her energies on other people would never have been an option.

How would Jack look now, she wondered curiously. Twenty years was a very long time and he would have aged. She hoped so, anyway. Life in California must have taken its toll – but she had also aged. Now she was in her sixties. Would he see her as an old woman? She hoped not. She had taken care of herself. Regular skin care, a good hairdresser, a moderate diet but possibly too little exercise.

'But I am still a good-looking woman,' she whispered. 'I can still turn heads. I have had my chances and more than one proposal.' She smiled at the memories. But then her expression changed as she wondered what *he* had done with *his* life. There must have been other women, she admitted, surprised at how much the idea hurt her. Jack Fratton without a woman was unthinkable. A leopard could not change its spots!

She sighed, blaming Larry Kline for his part in the disaster; blaming him for not marrying Ellen sooner. He should have whisked her to the altar but no – he allowed himself to be persuaded by Ellen's mother who protested that her daughter was too young at twenty. 'Why not wait another year?' she had suggested. 'There's all the time in the world.'

And so it had seemed until Jack had stolen away with her to Brighton, plied her with champagne and made her pregnant – setting in train a roller-coaster of events . . .

'Stop it, Alice!' she told herself. 'It's all in the past. The question now is how do I deal with Jack?' Whatever happened she must not let him know how much grief he had caused her over the intervening years. She must brush aside his apologies, if he offered any, and ignore any regrets he admitted. Perhaps she could wave a dismissive hand and say 'Good heavens, Jack, I never give it a thought these days!' and follow the words with a light laugh. Or she could say, 'You did me a great favour, Jack. I have thrived in the past twenty years!' On the other hand if Jack was going to pretend *he* had forgotten all about *her*, she might well demolish him with a few cutting remarks.

Alice, propped up against the pillows to take the strain from her heart, was trying to make herself comfortable when the ward doors swung open and she watched with interest as a new patient was wheeled in on a trolley propelled by two porters. They halted at the bed opposite Alice, where only the side curtains were drawn and Alice could easily watch the proceedings. For the next ten minutes there was a flurry of whispers and activity as the two night nurses installed her in the empty bed. They lifted her from the trolley on to the prepared mattress and then added a sheet and blanket and settled her with a few reassuring words. Another nurse brought a decanter of water and a glass to her bedside table and hung a chart on the bottom rail of the bed. Meanwhile the trolley had been wheeled away and the calm of the ward had not been disturbed.

One of the nurses patted the patient's shoulder and murmured, 'Sleep tight'.

'She can't hear you,' said the other nurse. 'She's unconscious.'

'Doctor Long says we can't be sure of that. Unconscious people can sometimes hear but can't respond.'

Was that true, Alice wondered, intrigued by the snippet as she watched them make their way back to the nurses' station. As the ward relapsed into a fragile silence Alice turned her mind once more to her own problems. She was still trying to decide what to say to Jack and how to deal with Fenella Anders, when she finally lost the thread of her thoughts and drifted into an exhausted sleep.

Later that day Izzie produced the key to their new flat and pushed open the door. 'After you,' she told her father. 'Bertie has promised he will carry me over the threshold! Isn't that romantic?'

'Very romantic.' He smiled. 'He gets top marks in the romance stakes!'

She followed him in and closed the door. 'Actually I had to drop a large hint before he thought of it. The passage is a bit narrow but it doesn't matter.' She threw open the door to a small parlour. 'It smells a bit of cats because the last tenant had three but once we move in we can open the windows wide and get in some fresh air. What do you think so far?'

'Very promising,' he lied. It was poky, he thought, but he must say nothing to spoil Izzie's pleasure. 'Nice fireplace.'

'It is, isn't it? We need to have the chimney swept but then we can blacklead it and use it and the landlord says it burns well except in very cold weather because of the down draught whatever that means. Theo and Cicely are giving us a companion set as a wedding present so we can keep the hearth tidy. There's nothing spoils a room more than a messy hearth.'

'I'm sure you're right.'

'It's made of brass. I could choose between that and copper but they both need cleaning and polishing so there isn't much difference – and I shall buy a better coal scuttle and put this one in the cupboard under the stairs. It has definitely seen better days.'

She opened the door to the understairs cupboard and pointed out the gas meter then led the way into the small kitchen-cum-scullery which looked out on to a neat garden – a patch of grass surrounded by narrow rockeries. 'There's a bit of a view into the gardens on either side but the fences give a bit of privacy. Bertie says the lawn is more like a pocket handkerchief but when we have a baby we can at least put the pram outside. Cicely says that we can borrow hers if her baby has outgrown it by then because Bertie's mother says we don't want to start a family too soon but we might. Who knows?'

Five minutes later, cutting short his encouraging comments about the garden, Isabel said, 'What has happened to your house in California? I suppose you do have one. Or you did. Is it a log cabin? Have you sold it?'

No one had yet asked him that question but he had prepared an answer. 'I left it until I knew whether or not I'd be staying here; whether or not I'd be welcome to stay. If I stay I'll sell it. It's not a house, it's a hotel.'

She was staring at him. 'You live in a hotel? You mean you don't have a home of your own?'

'I *own* the hotel and I live in it. There are private rooms.' To change the subject he asked, 'Aren't I going to see the bedrooms?'

She led the way but halfway up the stairs asked, 'How many bedrooms does it have, this hotel?'

'Five, not including the three rooms which are mine.'

She stared at him almost reproachfully. 'So you're rich?'

'Hardly rich. It's pretty ordinary. Clapboard. Small dining room.'

'We've only one bedroom here.' She opened the door. 'The other room is a box room which the landlady uses but we could store a few things in it. She lives on the top floor.' She waved a vague hand.

She seemed to be losing interest in the flat, he thought, wishing he had lied about his home.

Her expression had changed. 'It's easy for Theo and Cicely because her parents have given them a farm cottage. *Given* it to them.'

'But you'll be very happy here,' he said quickly. 'And more independent. It has a nice homely feel to it.' Seeing that she appeared unconvinced he went on. 'In a way it's nice to start small. When Bertie gets his promotion, and you've saved up a bit of money, you'll have the fun of looking for something a little bigger. I always loved having something to look forward to.'

'There is that,' Izzie agreed eagerly. 'I'm like you. I love looking ahead, too, waiting for the good things. I think I take after you in lots of ways.'

'Who knows!' he said as they went out again and Izzie locked the door behind them.

Maybe, he thought with a sigh. And then again, maybe not.

It was warm in the church that evening as late sunlight streamed in through the windows, throwing stripes of colour across a section of the pews. Olivia, Jack, and Isabel waited impatiently until the vicar arrived, five minutes late and flustered.

'You must forgive me,' he told them in some agitation. 'I had not forgotten our arrangement but was called out early this morning to a gentleman on the other side of the village. A gentleman requiring the last rites, poor fellow, and his wife was distraught, naturally, and quite alone. I had to wait until her son turned up to be with her.'

Jack stepped back a few paces and sat on one of the pews.

Olivia said, 'We quite understand. We have only been waiting a few—'

Isabel stepped forward impatiently. 'Well, now you are here we only need Bertie and he will be here in ten minutes so we can make a start on some things, I imagine.'

'Really?' he said, obviously taken aback by her brisk attitude. 'What exactly are you thinking of, Miss Fratton?'

'The flowers, for instance. Will the flowers be provided as usual or should we see to them? I would like them to be rather special and I thought that perhaps we could provide small posies, one for each end of the pews but only along the aisle and not on the ends where they won't be seen, I mean.'

Olivia frowned. 'Tie them on, do you mean?'

'Yes.'

'But they'll die without water.'

'Yes, but they'll last long enough to look pretty.'

The vicar looked dubious. 'Mrs Carrington from The Lodge House usually provides the flowers from her garden. Whatever is in bloom. It's very generous of her. If you want something more elaborate I think you will have to deal with them yourself, Miss Fratton.'

Olivia said, 'Don't you think you're running out of time, Izzie?'

Ignoring her comment, Isabel produced a small notebook and pencil and made a note in it. 'Next,' she said, 'I would like these hymns.' She handed the vicar a folded sheet of paper. 'And I think it would be nice if the choir sing the third one on the list and we just sit and listen.'

Olivia had expected to be consulted on various matters but now saw that her sister had everything organized, and she quietly moved to sit next to her father.

The vicar said, 'There is of course a small fee for the attendance of the choir. You really should have sorted all this out much earlier. The choir may not all be available but—'

Footsteps sounded outside and Bertie hurried in breathing heavily from the exertion of his ride. 'Sorry,' he muttered. 'I came as soon as I could.'

Isabel gave him a quick smile and made another note in her book. Then she held out her hand to him and drew him to stand beside her. 'Now we come to the bells,' she said. 'I'd like—'

The vicar said, 'There is another fee for the bells and actually it's a bit late for—'

'Good heavens!' She rolled her eyes. 'I had no idea that getting wed was so expensive, did you Bertie? But it has to be the most wonderful wedding because my father is here to give me away —' she threw him a radiant smile — 'and that is the best wedding present I could have!'

Nervously Jack raised his hand to advise the vicar of his presence but Olivia noted that he made no move to join them.

She said, 'We'd better introduce you,' and led him forward. The two men shook hands and the vicar said, 'So pleased you could get here in time,' and Jack muttered something non-committal.

Non-committal and somewhat brusque, thought Olivia, surprised.

The vicar smiled at Jack and said, 'I'm sure your daughter will be a beautiful bride. You must be very proud of her.'

Now Jack seemed lost for words and simply stared at the vicar. Was it guilt, Olivia wondered, for having abandoned them? Or fear, perhaps, of what people would say or think about him? Before she could decide, however, he nodded briefly, gave Olivia a shocked glance and hurried out of the church.

Isabel hid her surprise and forced a smile. 'He will also be my witness and will add his signature to ours when we sign the register after the ceremony.'

Bertie said, 'What exactly do you need me for, Izzie, because I have to be back at work in less than an hour and it will take me at least ten minutes on my bike to get back.'

Isabel hesitated. 'Well, I expect the vicar has some things to explain to us.' She looked at him expectantly.

'I do, yes.'

The vicar is mortified, thought Olivia, dismayed, because Izzie is taking over.

He said, 'Well now, let me see . . . It's usual to have the bride's family on this side –' he waved his hand – 'and the groom's on the other. The organist will be playing some suitable music while we await the entrance of the bride. Meanwhile we check that the best man has the ring so that there are no last minute panics.'

'That will be my brother Theo. He's very reliable.'

'I see. Yes, well, where was I?'

Olivia, thinking rapidly, said, 'Excuse me a moment,' and followed her father out of the church. Suppose he had run off again? Suppose his courage had failed and he . . .

'Over here!' he said.

He was leaning back against the church wall, one hand covering his eyes. For a moment she watched him, feeling an unexpected rush of sympathy for him and wondering if it was all too much for him. This so-called homecoming had not been easy, she thought, and he was probably deciding that he had made a big mistake by leaving whatever life he had had in California.

He's going to go back, she thought, surprised by how desolate that made her feel. She had never felt at all filial towards him but she had begun to warm to the man and had thought they might one day be friends. Sighing, she walked towards him and he lowered his hand and watched her approach, his expression anguished.

'I can't do this any longer!' He blurted the words out. 'You have to know something, Olivia. You have to know that . . .' He swallowed. 'You have to . . . understand that . . . Oh God!'

She laid a hand on his arm. 'You have to go back. I know. I think I knew all along that it would never work but I'm sorry we have made it so difficult for you. But it hasn't been easy for us – with the exception of Izzie.'

'No, Olivia.' He closed his eyes for a moment then opened them. 'You don't know, that's the whole point. I'm trying to tell you.' He took a deep breath. 'I lied to you.'

She stared at him. 'Lied? About what?' When he made no answer she said, 'About never marrying? You've got a wife somewhere. Is that it?' Her throat was dry and she realized she was close to tears. 'Once you knew that Mother was dead you—'

'No. That's not it.' He glanced nervously towards the church door. 'Look Olivia, don't ask me why I thought it was a good idea but . . . I was desperate to see you all even though—'

'Even though you wondered what sort of reception you'd get?'

'No.'

She frowned. 'You say you *lied* to us?'

He took a deep breath. 'I'm not Jack Fratton. I am not your father! You have to believe me.'

Vaguely they heard voices and Isabel's laugh rang out.

'Then . . . who are you?' The threatening tears had dried up to be replaced first by fear and then by anger. This man was nothing more than a common con-man! He was taking advantage of them. Somehow he had discovered . . .

'I'm Larry Kline.' He glanced towards the church porch but there was no sign of anyone emerging. He plunged on. 'I know it was ridiculous to think I could carry it through but at the time I wanted so much to see you all and to satisfy myself that—'

'Larry Kline?' Olivia felt as though the breath had been knocked out of her body. '*You are Larry Kline?*' For a moment she thought she might be sick and clutched her stomach as though she could in some way protect herself from what was to come.

He nodded. 'Please forgive me. It was a stupid idea but at the time it seemed . . . I was feeling low and I'd had a few drinks . . . It was very much spur of the moment stuff. I dashed off a letter to you and after that . . .'

She closed her eyes, afraid to even look at him. 'Then where is Father? What have you done to him? Where is the real Jack Fratton?'

'He died about five months ago. After I'd written to tell you I . . . I tore up the letter. I thought – hey! Why not? I could do it! I could pass myself off as—'

'Dead? Oh no!' Panic-stricken, Olivia clutched his arm. 'Don't tell Izzie! Not yet. Let her get through the wedding the way she has it planned. Please! It would be such a blow. We can tell her afterwards.'

He shook his head, unconvinced about the wisdom of allowing the deceit to go further. 'They used to say we looked like brothers and I thought, because you wouldn't know how he looks now – that is, how he *looked* before he died . . . I might just get away with it. Now I know. It was madness.'

Olivia's dazed mind was slowly beginning to grasp the enormity of what had happened. Larry Kline had impersonated his one-time friend. 'But why?' she asked, bewildered. 'Why not tell the truth?'

He searched the surrounding churchyard as if searching for words that would make his story sound more credible. 'Because I wanted to be part of the family and not just a visitor! Ellen was going to marry me. We were actually engaged. Until Jack . . . Well, something happened. I guess you can imagine! Then, when Ellen found she was expecting his child – that was Theo – she reluctantly agreed to marry him.' He looked at her with something akin to desperation. 'Don't you see? All these years . . . Ellen's children should have been *my* children. I should have been your father instead of Jack. You four should have been *my* family, not his! You should have been mine and Ellen's!'

Struggling to understand the full significance of his explanation it was Olivia's turn to close her eyes. She heard him say, 'Alice was in love with Jack. She was devastated. She never forgave him.'

Olivia opened her eyes. 'So that's why she never had a good word to say about him!' Her eyes widened as another thought struck her. 'So if Alice had come to the wedding you'd have been found out! She would have denounced you!'

He nodded. 'I'd lost track of how old she was and didn't take her into consideration . . . I can't believe I've been such an almighty fool! Whatever must you think of me?'

'I don't know what to think.' Olivia hesitated. 'I think I'm rather pleased – that you're not our father because we really are past the age where a father is important and now . . . Well, you can be a good friend. A sort of honorary uncle!' She laughed suddenly. 'If you were Jack Fratton then we'd always blame you for deserting us but if you're *not*, if instead you are the man that truly loved Mother, then we have nothing to forgive you for.'

He gave a wry smile but at that moment Bertie rushed out and grabbed his bicycle. 'I'm going to be late!' he cried. 'What a waste of time that was!' he added crossly as he cycled off.

'The thing is —' Olivia was thinking rapidly — 'I think we must keep this a secret until after the wedding. I'd hate to shatter Izzie's dream. After she's married she'll be more likely to take the news in her stride. She'll have Bertie. What do you think?'

It was agreed just in time as the vicar reappeared with Isabel and Olivia and 'Father' were told that the rehearsal was over.

The goodbyes were said and they went their separate ways. Isabel, buoyed up with excitement, chattered non-stop on the way home and fortunately quite failed to notice how quiet her two companions were.

Nine

What on earth am I supposed to do now? As the only one who knows the truth I am in something of a quandary. If I tell the family it will disrupt everything and cause no end of fuss. If I keep it to myself until later they will all blame me for not sharing the truth with them. Even Izzie . . .

Olivia, seated at the table in her bedroom, stared out into the garden but it was past eleven at night and heavy clouds shut out most of the light. She wore nothing but her nightdress and slippers but the room was warm and the small oil lamp bright enough to see by.

. . . Apart from being burdened with the secret, I am also unable to decide how I feel about it — about the fact that Father is not Father but Larry Kline, who has no real right to be here except as a family friend from the distant past. Part of me wants to strangle him but the other part is relieved that he does not belong here and can be asked, or told, to leave at any time . . .

Olivia yawned but she was not deceived into thinking that sleep would come easily to her when she settled down. Her thoughts wandered to her brother who had arrived home that evening looking very troubled. In answer to her questions he had simply said that 'things were coming to a head' and that 'matters were out of his hands'. Refusing to explain further he had stomped up to his room and remained there. Olivia sighed. Much as she wanted to help him she could not be all things to all people. Reluctantly she pushed his problems aside and returned to her main worry.

. . . Poor Larry! He could, of course, choose to leave at any time without a word of warning. He was very wrong to try and deceive us and worm his way into our lives and affections but it was also a great risk on his part and he must have been very keen to meet us. Not because of who we are but what we are — Ellen's children. Hardly

flattering to us but at least it shows how much he cared for Mother, which is in his favour. I wonder how different all our lives would have been if Mother had married him instead of Jack Fratton. We shall never know and we must never forget the debt we owe to Aunt Alice – even though, according to Jack – I mean Larry – she felt responsible for the way she chased out our father.

The strange thing is that now that I know who he really is I realize that I was warming to him in spite of my doubts and if he does leave I think I shall miss him. With Luke gone and Izzie married, I shall rattle around here. As nothing more than family friends, we might have jogged along here together. Who knows?

It was twenty past eleven that same night that Alice decided she must catch the attention of one of the nurses and waved her hand at a nurse who was passing the bed. 'Nurse Allington!' she called.

'Miss Redmond, you should be sleeping,' the nurse chided.

'I have to send a telegram,' Alice informed her briskly. 'I shall dictate it now and you must send it first thing – as soon as the Post Office opens. It is most urgent . . .'

'Miss Redmond!' The nurse paused, obviously reluctant to be delayed from the task in hand. 'It's the middle of the night! Your telegram can wait a while. You can send it first thing in the—'

'I tell you I want to deal with it now before I forget what I want to say. I may have confused the dates and it may be that the wedding is tomorrow and not the day after so they will have to alter it and wait for my arrival.'

The nurse, annoyed by Alice's attitude, tightened her lips. 'I fear your telegram *will* have to wait. It's hardly an urgent matter and here we are with a ward full of sick people who all need care and attention. Can you not see that a family telegram can wait until—'

'Where is Matron?' Alice glared at her indignantly. 'I would like to speak to—'

'Matron?' Her eyes widened with indignation. 'Well, did you ever hear the like! Matron, indeed! The poor woman will be fast asleep in her bed and no one will dare to disturb her. Now excuse me.'

She moved briskly away towards her next patient and Alice watched her go with rising fury. 'Uppity little madam!' she muttered, watching the nurse balefully as she bent over the bed and spoke with the patient, checked her temperature and moved on to someone further down the ward.

'Of all the impertinence!' she muttered with a despairing roll of her eyes. 'That's what you can expect from this genera- tion. Today's young women have no idea of discipline. None at all.' She sighed heavily as she settled back against the pillows, seething with annoyance. The carefully chosen words for her telegram had now slipped from her mind and she struggled to recapture them. Her heart was beginning to thump and Alice made an effort to calm herself. She did not want a repeat of the debacle on the train.

She took long, slow breaths but the discomfort in her chest did not lessen. Probably indigestion. The hospital food could have been better cooked. Milk of Magnesia would soon put her right.

She called 'Nurse!'

She raised her voice. '*Nurse!*'

The discomfort was spreading and becoming a pain. 'Oh! Not again!' she muttered, torn between fear and irritation. 'Nurse! Come at once!'

This time it was more of a plea than a command. At last she heard the sound of hurrying footsteps and the pain became something serious to worry about. She felt a rush of dizziness and someone was groaning. Was it her? Alice closed her eyes. Someone said, 'Quickly, fetch the superintendent!' and then Alice mercifully knew no more.

Breakfast the next morning found Lucas buttering toast and Olivia eyeing him uneasily over her scrambled eggs. His eyes were dark and his expression was something little short of despair.

'It's rude to stare!' he snapped.

'Forgive me. I was simply wondering—'

'Don't!'

'—if I could help. A listening ear. Two heads are better than one.'

'A friend in need?' At last he gave her a half-hearted grin.
'Yes.' She smiled. 'A shoulder to cry on.'

'For heaven's sake, Olivia! Can't a chap be miserable in
peace? I don't want your help or that pitying look!'

Ignoring his protests, Olivia pushed her plate away. 'Does
Aunt Alice know – about Fenella?'

'I wrote to her. She'll have it by now. She'll be very cross.'

'To put it mildly! Are you going to tell me what's happening?'
He was silent. 'Luke, I'd rather *not* know, if I'm honest,' she
admitted. 'I'll only worry more.'

He cut himself a slice of bread and reached for the marma-
lade. 'Then why do you ask?'

'In the hope that I can help you.'

'Fenella's had a letter – from her husband.' He avoided her
eyes, gazing down at the plate in front of him. 'It was what
she thought. He wasn't really with an ailing aunt, he was with
another woman.'

Olivia tried to hide her dismay. 'Is that good or bad?' she
asked in what she hoped was a neutral tone. 'I mean . . . are
you glad or sorry about that? And how does Fenella feel?'

'She's glad because he wants to live with the other woman.
To be precise, he wants Fenella to move out because he is still
the landlord and he wants his lady friend to move in with
him!' At last he lifted his gaze. 'It's going to set the tongues
wagging! And Fenella wants to move in with me . . . and I
want her to do just that.'

Deeply shocked by the revelations, Olivia was almost speech-
less – not because she had nothing to say but because she
didn't know how to put her reaction into words without
upsetting her brother. She could not bring herself to encourage
him in what seemed a very rash decision but he was not in
a mood to heed any warnings, and certainly not likely to
appreciate any advice.

After a long pause he sighed. 'Say something, for Lord's
sake!'

'I'm sorry, Luke. I don't know what to say. It all depends
on . . . It seems very sudden. Are you pleased that Fenella will
be free to do whatever the two of you decide? Is that what it
means to you? Will it mean a divorce? I just don't know about

these things, Luke.' She regarded him helplessly. 'Is it truly what you want? You'll have to tell me how you feel about it or how can I understand? How can I help you?'

'I don't know how I feel – except that I don't want her to spend another moment in his despicable company! I want her to move out of the pub.'

There was a long silence.

Olivia said, 'You do realize that your future in Cornwall with Aunt Alice—'

'She will probably disinherit me!'

'She will certainly try and change your plans. I doubt if she would countenance Fenella joining you down there.'

There was another silence.

He said, 'Aunt Alice can't run my life for me. I'm not a child.'

'Have you talked to Fenella about the Cornwall gallery and your future plans?'

'Naturally. She understands but we haven't thought it all through. It *is* rather sudden.' He ran anxious fingers through his hair. 'I shall talk to Father,' he said. 'That's what they're for, isn't it? Fathers. To give advice to their sons. He's a man of the world. He might know what we should do.'

He might, she thought wryly, though he's not your father . . . but he probably could advise you. Not that he has made a big success of his own life! She said, 'That's a good idea.'

'Has he come down yet?'

'He had a slice of toast earlier and went out for a walk. He says it clears his head.'

'So can Fenella stay here?'

'It's fine with me, and you won't object, and Isabel will be moving out tomorrow.' She glanced towards the stairs. 'Talk of the devil!'

Izzie appeared, already washed and dressed. She smiled brilliantly at them both. 'Miss Denny will be here in ten minutes for any final alterations although I have tried not to eat more or less than usual so the dress should still fit perfectly. She is so happy. She says my dress is the best she has ever made and I shall be her most beautiful bride! And I'm not to mind if she cries during the service because they'll be tears of happiness.'

Lucas said, 'And you will be beautiful.'

'Oh that's so sweet!' Surprised, Isabel beamed at him. Blissfully unaware of his state of mind she cut a slice of bread, buttered it and went on. 'So where's Father?'

'Gone for a walk to clear his head.' Lucas pushed his plate away and stood up and winked at Olivia. 'I'm sure you two have lots to talk about.'

Olivia stifled a groan. 'We have,' she agreed, wondering whether she should mention Fenella to Isabel and quickly deciding that that was her brother's problem.

She was on the point of leaving the table when she glanced from the window and saw a boy on a bicycle dismounting beside their gate. Instinctively she put a hand to her heart. 'It's a telegram boy!'

Isabel leaped to her feet in alarm and for a moment they were both silent, watching his jaunty progress towards the front door. Olivia rushed from the dining room and opened the front door.

'Telegram, missus!' The boy, probably no more than fourteen, smiled cheerfully. With a flourish, he handed over a buff-coloured envelope, thrust his hands into his pocket and began to whistle.

'Oh Lord!' Isabel's face paled. Nine times out of ten a telegram meant bad news. She opened the envelope with shaking fingers. 'Oh no!' she cried, scanning the neat rows of capital letters. 'It's Aunt Alice. She's in St Barts Hospital in London. She's had a heart attack!'

They stared at each other. Isabel recovered first. 'In *London*? What on earth is she doing in London?'

'A heart attack!' Badly shaken, Olivia leaned back against the door jamb.

Ignoring their reaction to the bad news, the telegram boy said perkily, 'Any answer?'

The sisters looked at each other. Olivia wondered fleetingly how they chose the telegram boys. Not for their sensitivity, that was clear. She said, 'I'll have to go up on the next train and see how she is and find out what's happening.'

Isabel gasped. 'But what about the wedding? When will you be back?'

'I have no idea until I see her and speak to the doctor. If she's fit enough I'll have to bring her home somehow.'

'I can't come with you,' Isabel said quickly. 'I've got to see Miss Denny.'

'I'll manage somehow.'

Olivia looked at the waiting boy. 'There's no answer but wait and I'll fetch you a sixpence.'

Moments later they watched him remount, still whistling as he rode away.

'Bad news?'

Olivia turned to see that Larry had returned from the opposite direction. 'I'm afraid so. I have to go up to London on the next train. Izzie will explain.'

He said, 'I'll ring for a taxi to take you to the station – or I could come with you if I would be of any help.'

Remembering that Lucas wanted to speak to him, Olivia declined his offer but agreed that it would help if he called a taxi for her.

Miss Denny chose that moment to arrive and as they all milled about in the hall Lucas joined them, looking for his father.

For one long moment Olivia was suddenly and heartily thankful that she was needed in London and was going to escape the family for a few hours.

As soon as Olivia reached the hospital she made her way to the front desk where a small wooden plate gave the receptionist's name as Mrs Burrows.

Olivia managed a smile. 'Good morning. I have received a telegram from a Doctor Long who says that Miss Alice Redmond was brought here yesterday as an emergency patient.'

'Which ward would that be then?' Elderly, Mrs Burrows fixed Olivia with stern blue eyes and pursed lips.

'I'm afraid I don't know. The telegram was very brief.'

Mrs Burrows sighed and turned away with a slight shake of her head. She riffled through an index tray and nodded. 'Miss Alice Redmond?'

'Yes.'

She studied the card and then pointed towards a flight of stairs.

'Turn left at the top and after fifty yards or so turn right and the doors to the ward are on your left. You can't miss it. Any one of the staff will help you.'

Olivia had never been in hospital and she was already feeling nervous, affected by the smell of disinfectant, the murmur of concealed voices and the echoing clatter of footsteps along corridors and up and down the stairs. The busy hum of London's traffic was muffled and Olivia had the feeling that she had stepped into another world – an alien world where she would find Aunt Alice taking a new role. No longer in charge of her destiny but brought down by illness.

Once inside the appropriate ward she was at once approached by a nurse who smiled enquiringly and introduced herself as Nurse Watson.

'I'm looking for a Miss Alice Redmond—' Olivia began.

'Ah yes! You were summoned, I believe.' She tutted. 'Miss Redmond would not eat any breakfast until a telegram had been dispatched to you. Doctor Long was rather annoyed. She has had a mild heart attack although she refuses to accept the fact.' She indicated a bed near the nurses' station. 'She's over there behind the curtains. Last time I looked in she was awake. You can talk to her for ten minutes – unless you want to speak with the doctor in which case you will have to wait more than an hour as he is busy on another ward with his students.'

'I think I'll speak to her now. We have a family wedding tomorrow and I shall have to get back later today or my sister will also be having a heart attack!' She laughed but the nurse was obviously not amused.

She led the way to Alice's bed and pulled back the curtains. 'You have a visitor, Miss Redmond,' she said in a firm tone. 'But there is to be no talk of you discharging yourself until the doctor has given his permission.'

Alice threw back the bedcovers but the nurse darted forward. 'Stay where you are, Miss Redmond! You know what Doctor Long told you.' She turned to Olivia. 'Miss Redmond is not a good patient, I fear. Too wilful by far. You are allowed ten minutes. Please see that the patient stays in bed and don't allow her to become excited or I shall have to ask you to leave.'

Alice looked very pale and her eyes seemed to have sunk into their sockets. She looked at least ten years older, thought Olivia, trying to hide her dismay. This frail, fretful creature was unfamiliar to her.

Before she could speak Alice said loudly, 'I want my clothes. They have taken my clothes!'

'They are quite safe, Miss Redmond and *if* – and it's a big "if" – you are allowed to leave your bed, your clothes will be returned to you.'

Alice watched the nurse walk away then turned imperiously towards her visitor. 'Find out where they have taken my clothes, Olivia, and fetch them for me. I intend to discharge myself and no one can stop me. You must call a taxi and we will travel down to Canterbury together. I shall be perfectly comfortable. Every taxi carries a rug for the knees.'

'But you are probably not fit enough to—'

'Let me be the judge of that!' She glared at Olivia. 'I have to talk to Lucas before he totally ruins his life. Fenella indeed! I've never heard of such nonsense. She will soon discover that she is no match for me and Luke will realize that she is not worth his throwing away a glittering career.'

Olivia sat down on the bedside chair. 'You do realize, don't you, that it's Isabel's wedding tomorrow? We shall all be very distracted and—'

'Wedding or no wedding, I intend to talk to Lucas and put him straight about Fenella. Don't try and change my mind, Olivia. You know me better than that.' A touch of colour had appeared in her cheeks and Olivia recalled the nurse's warning.

'Please don't get excited, Aunt Alice. You have to take care of—'

'Oh do stop fussing! You always were a worrier!' She made another effort to slide from the bed but Olivia prevented her.

'I shall call the nurse back if you don't behave yourself!' she said. 'You know it's for your own good.'

Reluctantly her godmother gave in but a sulky expression took over her face. 'I didn't think you were so bossy, Olivia. She's only a nurse and I shall speak directly to Doctor Long when he arrives. Then we shall see!'

'Wouldn't it be better if you remain here for a few days and then came down to talk to Luke after the wedding?'

'No it would not. I've already told you what I intend to do. Now go and find my clothes and bring them to me then ring for a taxi.' Suddenly breathless, she put a hand to her chest. 'You see what you have done? You're upsetting me!'

Olivia closed her eyes and counted to ten. Her mind was racing. Did she want the doctor to discharge Alice, she wondered. Her aunt appeared very fragile and hardly up to a long journey by taxi . . . And then when they reached home she would no doubt quarrel with Luke and that might bring on another attack. Staring down at her aunt Olivia had another thought. How would Aunt Alice react when she came face to face with Larry?

'Get along, Olivia, and find my clothes. You can't expect me to travel in this ridiculous hospital gown.'

Taking her chance, Olivia nodded and made her way out of the ward, her thoughts spinning and her head beginning to ache.

Outside the ward she hesitated, wishing that Doctor Long would somehow materialize and tell her what she should do but instead a nurse appeared and eyed her enquiringly.

Olivia explained briefly what was happening and the nurse tutted.

'I'm afraid your aunt is too self-willed for her own good!' she told Olivia. 'You might find Doctor Long in his office – first on the right, third door on the left. You can't miss it. If he agrees that she can go home I'll find her clothes for you and the reception will call a taxi.'

Olivia had the feeling that the hospital would be quite happy to see the back of her aunt. On her way to the office, Olivia found her way blocked by a woman in a wheelchair surrounded by a small group of people who might be members of her family. The woman apparently had the opposite problem to Aunt Alice – she was insisting that they had no right to discharge her when she was still ill.

'But they must know, Ma,' one of the younger women protested. 'If they say you're cured then you're cured! You can't just stay on. They need your bed for someone else.'

The young man pushing the wheelchair nodded. 'It's a hospital, Ma, not a hotel!'

Finding Doctor Long's office, Olivia knocked and was told to enter. Small and decidedly round, the doctor was not quite what she had expected but, seated at his desk, he adjusted his spectacles on a small nose and peered up at her through small brown eyes.

'Doctor Long, I'm worried about Alice Redmond who is my godmother and who is—'

He was already nodding. 'Ah yes! The heart attack patient and rather troublesome if I may say so.' He smiled to soften the words. 'She will be discharged tomorrow or the next day, when I think she is strong enough.'

'She's demanding I fetch her clothes . . .'

'I don't doubt it but I can assure you she will not be discharged today – clothes or no clothes!'

'I'm finding it difficult to convince her that—'

'Then don't. Go home and leave her with us. We are used to these arguments, Mrs – er, you didn't give me your name.'

'It's Miss. Miss Fratton.'

'Go straight home, Miss Fratton. I shall tell her you were sent away on my orders. She is not to be bothered by visitors! Telephone us tomorrow around eleven for a further progress report.'

Olivia frowned. 'We have a family wedding tomorrow. No one would be free to come up and fetch her.'

'A wedding? How splendid! Then you won't be able to deal with a fractious old woman!' He beamed at her. 'Leave her with us. She'll be in good hands and she needs rest, not excitement. She may believe that she is fit to attend a wedding but I assure you she is not.'

Olivia reflected that the wedding would be the least of her worries if Aunt Alice came face to face with Fenella or Larry but she felt vaguely treacherous at thus colluding to thwart her godmother's plans.

'Thank you, doctor.' Olivia, only partly reassured, gave in gratefully. 'Then I'll . . .' She hesitated.

'Just slip away, Miss Fratton.' Doctor Long stood up, gathering papers from the desk and shuffling them into a manageable pile which he then rolled and fastened with an elastic band, clearly signalling that the short interview was at an end.

Olivia preceded him from the room, said goodbye and pushed her doubts to the back of her mind. She took a deep breath, hurried back the way she had come and gratefully 'slipped away'.

Arriving back home two hours later Olivia was about to put her key in the lock of the front door when it opened and Miss Denny came out. She looked flustered and indignant and glared at Olivia.

'Really, Miss Fratton, I'm astonished that you could abandon your sister on the eve of her wedding!' she told Olivia, drawing herself up to her full height. 'Poor Isabel is quite beside herself and no wonder. Your place was here! That poor girl. Tears before her wedding! That's a terrible omen! Can you imagine anything worse?'

Olivia began to say that she could – that she could imagine Isabel's godmother dying alone in a London hospital, which would certainly cast a deep shadow over the proceedings – but Miss Denny rushed on.

'I've stayed as long as I could, trying to be of some comfort, trying to pour oil on troubled water, but meanwhile you go gallivanting up to London . . .'

Breathlessly, she fell silent and tried to push her way past Olivia but the latter caught her arm. 'Isabel's godmother is in hospital after a heart attack,' she said angrily. 'Didn't my sister tell you?'

'No she did not. She was too busy quarrelling with her brother and you might well ask why! Did you know that he is planning to invite Fenella Anders to the wedding against Isabel's wishes? That is *Mrs* Fenella Anders!' She clutched her chest which was heaving with righteous indignation. 'The village is full of it. You had no right to allow him to invite that woman into the church . . . to intrude on a service of Holy Matrimony.'

Olivia said, 'I'm not aware that any of this is your business, Miss Denny, but perhaps you would remember that I am not Lucas's mother nor am I Isabel's mother and I am doing my best to deal with everything and . . .' Her voice began to shake ominously. Oh Lord! I'm going to cry, she thought, panic-stricken. Once I start I shall never stop.

At that moment she was aware of a firm hand on her arm and turned to see Larry, his face full of concern. He turned to Miss Denny and said firmly, 'You've been very kind, Miss Denny, but now Olivia is back I think we can manage.'

Miss Denny wavered but then drew herself up. 'Of all the hypocritical things to say! Perhaps if you had returned when you should have done, to look after your family—'

Hastily Olivia intervened. 'Thank you for your help, Miss Denny, but I think you should go now before you say something you may regret.'

The dressmaker still had things she wanted to say but there was now a look in Olivia's eyes which deterred her. She said, 'Well then. I'll say no more!' With a final icy look in Olivia's direction she turned and walked away, her back stiff with disapproval.

Larry slid a comforting arm round Olivia's shoulders. 'Good to see you back. It's been chaos but the kettle's boiling and Isabel is supposed to be making a pot of tea.'

Olivia said, 'I wonder if Aunt Alice *will* come tomorrow. She's been invited.'

He shrugged. 'Her choice!'

Olivia closed her eyes, willing away the tears that would betray her if she allowed them to do so. She found Isabel sitting alone, dabbing at her eyes with a damp handkerchief.

Isabel glanced up balefully. 'You stayed in London for ages!'

'Your godmother is in a poor way,' Olivia snapped. 'Thank you for asking after her!'

'Oh . . . good. Is she coming to the wedding? Because if she is she will find Fenella and—'

'I doubt if she will be well enough. Where's Luke?'

'Gone to fetch his lady friend!'

'Do stop it, Izzie!'

'She's not invited but he's determined to bring her. I never thought he could be so selfish. Miss Denny thinks he's—'

Olivia snapped, 'Miss Denny should mind her own business!'

'Miss Denny's on my side!' A resentful expression settled on her face. 'You don't care. Nobody does.' Her voice shook. 'I hate this family. I really do! I sometimes wish I'd never been born!'

Larry said sharply, 'Don't say that. Your mother gave her life for you! I'm sure she adored you.'

'How would you know? You weren't here!'

'I'm sorry. Your father should have been here for you.'

She stared at him, eyes wide with indignation. 'How do you dare say such a thing?' she demanded. 'It was up to you but you didn't come back. It seemed as if you didn't care about me.'

'I . . . *He* should have . . .' Stricken by his slip, he glanced at Olivia for help.

'Please!' Olivia, disconcerted by the direction of the conversation, glanced fearfully at her sister but Isabel seemed oblivious of Larry's confusion. 'You have to stop this, Isabel. Things happen that are nobody's fault. People make wrong decisions and then it's impossible to change things; impossible to put things right. No one can turn the clock back and reinvent the past. You have to rise above it – for Bertie's sake if not your own. It's his wedding day, you know, as well as yours.'

'It's easy for you to say that but if you were in my shoes . . .' She sniffed. 'Everything's going wrong.'

'No it isn't. All along you wanted one thing for your wedding day – that your father could be here to give you away and—' She broke off abruptly. She had intended to say 'here he is' but that was a lie. At some time in the future the truth would emerge and Isabel would probably resent the deceit for the rest of her life. If, however, she was told the truth now she would be devastated. It was an impasse. Shocked and helpless she stared at her sister but Isabel had jumped to her feet.

'I'm going over to see Bertie,' she announced. 'At least his family are on my side.'

'It's not a matter of taking sides!' Olivia's voice was rising in spite of her determination to stay calm. 'This isn't a war, Isabel!'

'It feels like one to me!' She ran from the kitchen and as

Olivia moved to run after her, they heard the front door open and slam.

Larry shrugged. 'Let her go. They'll put it down to nerves. They'll make the right soothing noises.'

'Do you think so? I hope you're right.'

'Now tell me what happened at the hospital.'

Less than an hour later Lucas appeared at the back door holding Fenella by the hand. She looked apprehensive and Olivia felt sorry for her. What an unpleasant situation she had been drawn into!

Lucas said, 'Is Aunt Alice here?'

Olivia held open the door and said, 'Come in both of you,' and smiled at Fenella. To her brother she said, 'As far as I know Aunt Alice will have to remain at the hospital so I'm not expecting her to appear.'

They came in almost reluctantly and she saw that Lucas was carrying a bag which presumably contained Fenella's clothes. He said, 'Fenella's going to have my room. I'll manage somewhere else,' and slid his free arm round her waist. Looking round he asked where Isabel was hiding.

'She's gone over to be with Bertie for a while. Finding us all rather troublesome.' She smiled.

Fenella said, 'I'm quite happy to stay here and not come to church but Lucas—'

'She's coming to church with me or else neither of us are going to be there!' He glared at Olivia as though somehow she was responsible for the difficulties.

Olivia felt like screaming but instead she nodded. 'Do whatever feels right for you.'

Larry chose that moment to return from wherever he had been. He smiled at Lucas and shook hands with Fenella. 'Call me Jack,' he told her. 'I think we met at the Coach and Horses when you showed me Luke's painting.'

'Of the cathedral. I remember.'

Olivia and Larry watched the two young people set off upstairs then exchanged a look of mutual sympathy.

Olivia smiled uncertainly. 'I am beginning to give up hope,' she confessed. 'Will the time ever come when Isabel's wedding is in the past and we can start our lives again? It seems to have been looming over us forever!'

Larry laughed. 'I promise you the time will come – and then you and I will have a talk about the future. We do have a future, you know, Olivia.' He looked at her earnestly.

She sighed. 'Life goes on. I know. That's what I tell myself but . . .' She shrugged. 'I can't quite see where mine is going. It's always been the family – the four of us – rattling along together but after tomorrow . . .' Her voice wavered and she blinked rapidly. She had promised herself that she would put all her doubts to one side and devote herself to the wedding and now here was Jack undermining her, albeit unintentionally.

Seeing how fragile she was feeling he said quickly, 'But that's for us to think about next week, when we've recovered from all the excitement.' He winked at her. 'There's safety in numbers and I have a great plan for the two of us.'

Now she stared at him. 'You mean that you're staying here?'

He shook his head, grinning, watching her expression. 'Not on your life! I mean I'm going back to California and you're coming with me!'

Startled, Olivia stared at him. Was he seriously suggesting taking her to America? She stammered, 'Oh no! I mean I couldn't. I'll be quite happy here. Mrs Whinnie has offered me a job as her companion.'

She began to explain the connection but he held up his hand.

'I don't see you as a companion, Olivia.'

'I'll be near to Isabel and Theo and I'll always be welcome in Cornwall with Luke and Fenella.'

Before he could reply there was a rush of footsteps at the side of the house and Theo appeared at the back door, a broad grin on his face. 'Congratulations, Auntie Olivia!' he cried, hugging her. 'You now have a little niece! And you, Father, have been promoted to Grandfather!' Smiling broadly, the two men shook hands. 'Cicely sends her love and says you must come round in the morning and see the little one.' He glanced round the kitchen. 'So where is everyone?'

Olivia rolled her eyes. 'A good question!' She laughed. 'Izzie has gone round to see Bertie and Lucas is upstairs with Fenella!'

'Ah! Do I detect problems?' Stunned by the fact of father-hood, he seemed unfazed by the prospect.

'Nothing we can't solve,' she told him with more hope than conviction and hurried to the stairs to call Luke and Fenella down to hear the good news.

It was just before midnight that her footsteps stopped outside Luke's room and Isabel hesitated, glancing back along the poorly lit passage as though uncertain what to do next. She knew that Fenella was sleeping in Luke's room but was her brother with her? If he was it would make her mission twice as awkward. Crossing her fingers she took a deep breath and tapped appre-hensively on the door. There was no answer and she had raised her hand to knock more loudly when the door opened and Fenella stared out at her. Obviously surprised by her visitor Fenella said defensively, 'If you want me to say I won't be at the wedding you needn't ask because I won't be there – which means that Luke won't be there either!'

'Are you alone?'

Fenella nodded.

'May I come in?'

Glancing down, Fenella saw that her visitor was barefooted and dressed only in a nightdress and shawl.

Silently she opened the door further, allowing Isabel to enter. She then retreated to the bed and sat down. 'If it's Luke you want he's downstairs, sleeping on the sofa.'

'It's not Luke. It's you.' Unsure how to start, Isabel crossed to the window and glanced outside. 'The clouds are clearing,' she said. 'It might be fine tomorrow.'

'That's all that matters then!' Fenella snapped. 'As long as the weather is fine for your wedding – that's all you care about, isn't it? You don't care if you make people unhappy. You don't worry about your godmother who's in hospital . . . you don't appreciate your sister who's worrying herself to a shadow trying to make everything right for your big day!' Her voice rose. 'You don't understand that Luke is tying himself in knots for someone he loves – me! You have a newborn baby in the family—'

'I was with Bertie but I'll—'

'—but you haven't said a word about him!'

Stung by the accusations, Isabel turned from the window. 'You're hardly perfect! Pushing your way into this family, upsetting us, getting the Frattons talked about in the village . . .'

'Since when did a little gossip hurt anyone?'

'They've been gossiping about you and Luke. Does *that* hurt? Because it hurts us! We don't care to be the subject of gossip!'

'I should think you'd be used to it by now! They started whispering about the Frattons years ago when your father ran off!'

Isabel closed her eyes, holding back a furious reply, reminding herself that she had promised her father that she would 'mend fences', as he had put it.

Unaware, Fenella reached for the bedspread and wrapped herself in it as though to protect herself from the harsh words that would follow.

'It hurts *us*,' Isabel told her in a quieter tone, 'because it risks Luke's future and his career! Aunt Alice is going to disapprove of you, and Luke depends on her goodwill. If you love Luke you should bear that in mind.'

There was a tense silence as they glared at one another.

'This is getting us nowhere.' Fenella sighed heavily. 'What do you want exactly, Isabel? Why are you here? I'd like to get some sleep.'

Isabel hesitated. 'I came to apologize, if you must know.' She rushed on before Fenella could reply. 'I know what you're thinking – that it didn't sound much like an apology, but that's because you didn't give me a chance. I came to say you are invited to the wedding and I'm sorry about everything . . . about you and your husband . . .' Isabel faltered. She was making a mess of everything and she had promised Father.

Fenella watched her curiously. 'This is all a bit sudden, isn't it?' She had tucked her legs under her and was staring up at Isabel from the rumpled bed and looked much younger than she was.

Isabel sat down on a nearby chair. 'I've been talking to my father,' she said with a touch of pride in her voice. 'He means a lot to me and I . . . I was getting very confused and unhappy and I had nobody to talk to except Olivia who . . . well, she's only my sister and she's not much older than me.'

Fenella raised her eyebrows. 'Luke says she wants to help you but you won't listen to her.'

Ignoring this unwelcome truth, Isabel leaned forward and clasped her hands around one knee. 'Father's different. He—'

'He's hardly perfect either – as fathers go!'

Stopped in her tracks, Isabel considered this slur and ignored that too. 'Father doesn't want me to have any regrets later about my wedding day and he wants it to be the happiest day of my life and as he says, how can it be if you and I and Luke are at loggerheads? He's right, I know, but it's not simply that. I mean, if you marry Luke, and I expect you will, you'll be part of the family.'

'So you're only doing it to please your father?'

'Not the way you mean! No! Truly, Fenella,' she went on earnestly, 'I could see it quite clearly when he explained it. He's a really wonderful man! I was already wishing that things were different between you and me for Luke's sake – that is I didn't want us to be at odds but I couldn't bring myself to face the truth until Father explained it.' She waited for Fenella's response but when none came she shrugged. 'Oh dear! I'm getting this all wrong, aren't I?'

Fenella drew the bedspread closer round her shoulders and said nothing.

Isabel said, 'I do want us to be friends. You'll be my sister-in-law after tomorrow. Father says families are important—'

'And blood's thicker than water!' She drew a sharp breath. 'Luke said you could be unpredictable.'

Isabel frowned. Was that a compliment, she wondered. She made a last attempt and moved from the chair to stand beside the bed; then she held out her hands. 'Could we start again, do you think?'

Seconds ticked by and after a heart-stopping delay Fenella took the outstretched hands in hers, smiled suddenly and nodded. 'We could certainly try,' she said.

Ten

The ward just after two o'clock in the morning was eerie in the subdued lighting and full of the usual sounds – patients snoring, coughing, tossing in discomfort or calling out in their sleep – and Nurse Allington kept her voice low.

'Mrs Adams might need a sleeping draught,' she told her colleague, 'and Miss Bradley in the far right bed, poor soul, will almost certainly need a bed pan before the night is out.'

The night nurse, new on the ward and still doing her training, lowered her voice, glancing uneasily along the row of beds. 'What about that Miss Redmond? What shall I say if she starts demanding . . .?'

'Pretend not to hear her. I'm afraid to say she has exhausted my patience. She's a very selfish woman who expects constant attention. She seems to think that she is the only patient on the ward.' Exasperated, she rolled her eyes. 'If she asks me once more to fetch her clothes I shall—'

'But she might need something – that is, something else like a drink of water or . . .' She frowned in the direction of Miss Redmond's bed. 'I think she's waving her hand now.'

'I'd not put it past her but her carafe has been refilled and she has had her pills.'

'And if she wants help to go to the lavatory?'

'That's quite different – but she doesn't. I took her to the toilet not twenty minutes ago. But of course, when she does need to go, you must take her there and bring her back but try not to lose sight of her. She's determined to discharge herself against the doctor's advice. And don't get into any arguments, nurse. Last time she called for me it was to bring her clothes and send for a cab! She has a way with words and could talk the hind legs off a donkey but it's not good for her and the doctor wants her to stay calm!'

'She *is* waving.' She peered through the gloom. 'She's sort of beckoning.'

Nurse Allington tutted. 'She'll soon settle down. Doctor Long is adamant that she must not be allowed to discharge herself and most certainly not in the middle of the night!' She gathered some reports. 'It looks as though she has gone to sleep at last.' She smiled. 'Think yourself lucky! I'll take these reports to the superintendent.'

'Nurse! I need a bed pan!' Miss Bradley's querulous voice was high with anxiety.

Nurse Allington gave a short laugh. 'There you are! What did I say? See to the poor soul, nurse, and I'll be back soon.' She hurried away towards the swing doors and was gone.

Sighing, the nurse hurried to fetch a bed pan and on the way back saw that Miss Redmond was at last silent. She whispered a promise to another patient, who complained loudly that her sleeping draught was not working, that she would be with her directly. The night shift had begun in earnest.

The morning of Isabel's wedding dawned with a frisky wind but clear blue skies and Olivia uttered a prayer of heartfelt thanks. One less problem for Isabel, she thought as she pushed aside the covers and thrust her feet into her slippers. As she was pulling on her dressing gown there was a knock at the door and Isabel appeared.

'I just wanted to know for sure . . .' she faltered. 'I know you will think me quite mad but . . . is Papa still here?'

Olivia stared at the pale face. 'Still here? But of course he . . . What makes you ask that?'

'I just wondered. I want to be sure before I allow myself to be excited. I knew you wouldn't understand but . . .' She was almost wringing her hands.

Olivia gave her a reassuring hug but her sister's fears had nevertheless put a small doubt into her mind. 'We'll find out,' she said and, leading the way, knocked on Larry's door. She called, 'Time to get up! The big day has arrived!'

A loud groan and creaking bed springs assured them that he was still with them and a huge smile lit up Isabel's face as she returned to her room. Olivia hurried to the kitchen to start the breakfast which today would be very frugal – porridge and toast and a large pot of tea.

Thirty minutes later the family were gathered round the kitchen table – Isabel, in high spirits; Fenella and Luke very much wrapped up in themselves; Olivia anxious as a mother hen and Larry, whom she thought somewhat subdued, but forcing a cheerful expression.

Isabel, now flushed with excitement, said, 'I wish Theo was here with us, and Mother. Then we would be a complete family sitting round the table for the first time ever.'

Fenella said, 'I'm sure your mother is with us in spirit.' She sipped her tea and added, 'Would you like me to brush your hair, Izzie, and pin it up for you?'

Izzie? Inwardly delighted, Olivia hid her surprise but her sister accepted the offer gracefully, adding, 'But we'd better make a start and finish it before Miss Denny arrives.'

Luke said, 'Fenella and I are going to visit Theo and Cicely – just a short visit to see the new baby but we'll be back in time to give you a helping hand.' He glanced at Olivia. 'I'm hoping Aunt Alice won't make a surprise appearance.'

Isabel's eyes widened fearfully. 'Oh no! That would ruin everything. Oh she couldn't, could she?'

'Most unlikely. The doctor is determined not to release her for a few days more even though I can imagine she is being a thorough nuisance. So eat up, everyone. I want to have breakfast out of the way so we can concentrate on getting ready.'

As the hands of the church clock reached four Isabel stood at the church entrance with Larry, her heart thudding with disbelief. This was her wedding day and her father was there with her – a long-held dream that she had never thought would come true. Her arm was through his and when she turned her head he smiled and winked at her.

The little church held a congregation of twenty-two people and as Isabel waited for the musical cue that they were to start their walk down the aisle, she picked out those she loved most from among the visitors ranged in front of the altar steps. Theo was there by kind permission of his wife and new baby and Olivia was there next to Luke who had his arm round Fenella. Miss Denny, as planned, had chosen to sit to one side. On the other side of the church Bertie's parents stood side by side, Dorcas already weeping into her handkerchief, and there were some others of their family as yet unknown to Isabel.

As the organist struck the first notes and the bride, her face aglow, walked slowly down the aisle, the telegram boy discovered that at Laurel House there was no one at home. Disappointed that there would be no tip, he slipped the telegram through the letter box and went on his way.

As Dorcas Hatterly put her handkerchief away, Luke squeezed Fenella's hand and Olivia breathed a deep sigh of relief; the bride and groom shyly exchanged their rings. Larry Kline admitted to himself that his initial deceit had been a bad mistake but that, by some miracle, it had turned out well. At least for the moment, he amended silently. Eventually there would be a reckoning!

Later, the little company celebrated, the speeches were made and applauded, and the wedding was declared a huge success by all present. Only Olivia had to force her smile as the fateful telegram waited beneath the mantelpiece clock; only she knew that Alice Redmond had died during the previous night.

Two days later Luke was on his way to Newquay and Fenella was making arrangements to follow him. Alice's body was to be sent down there the following day and held briefly in a local funeral parlour which she had specified in her will. The affairs of the gallery could not be left without a guiding hand and, although it had closed for three days as a mark of respect, Luke knew that Alice would have laid down strict instructions which involved passing the ownership of the gallery into his hands.

There was also the matter of her funeral, all of which she had planned with meticulous care, and Olivia and Isabel would also attend. In the meantime Laurel House felt empty and Olivia was grateful for Larry's presence.

They were sitting over a late breakfast next morning when Larry finished his toast and said, 'I meant what I said, Olivia. I think the best thing for both of us is to settle in California. Have you given the idea any thought?'

Olivia almost choked on her toast. She had dreaded this

moment and she *had* given the matter some thought but she had reached no conclusion. 'I thought you might stay here,' she said. 'Isabel has taken it for granted that you will.'

Larry shook his head. 'This isn't about Isabel or Luke or Theo. This is about you and me – and I have a life back home. I thought I might be needed here but Ellen's family is fine – except for you and I think you would be happy out there with me instead of here on your own.'

She shook her head. 'Something might go wrong and who would they turn to if I were in California?'

'They would deal with their own problems. They're adults, Olivia. They're not meant to rely on you. I reckon you've done your share . . . and please don't mention Mrs Whinnie. It was a reasonable idea if you were desperate for money but you're worth much more than that. If you come back with me you'll have your own room in the hotel and I'll teach you how to run it and when I pop off it will be yours.' He grinned suddenly. 'Am I anywhere near tempting you?'

'But I have to tell them the truth about you and . . .' She regarded him unhappily.

'No you don't. That's my job. I'll write to them when I'm good and ready – but all you have to worry about is whether you're coming to California with me or staying here.'

Olivia began to collect the plates but Larry put a hand over hers. 'Leave them! There's no way you're going to slide off and start washing up until we've settled this.' He sat back in his chair and looked at her. 'What do you think Ellen would say if you could ask her? D'you think she'd trust me to look after you?'

She hesitated, startled by the question.

'D'you think she'd have come to California with me if I'd asked her to, all those years ago – if Jack hadn't messed every-thing up for all of us?'

'You can't expect me to decide just like that! It's a big step!'

'Then take a big step! Why not?' He leaned forward, grin-ning. 'It's your turn, Olivia. Your brothers and sisters won't begrudge you your chance at a new life. They each have a new life. They can't begrudge you the same chance.'

Olivia was beginning to wonder where Larry thought their

life together would lead. Surely he was not imagining that they could live together as man and wife, and if not then what would her position be? She was not his daughter and she hoped he had no plans to pretend she was but it was a rather embarrassing thing to ask about.

As if reading her mind he said, 'You would simply be the daughter of a friend. That's what you are, Olivia. It's quite simple.'

'But it might happen – although I doubt it will – that I meet someone . . . that is, I mean a man. What would happen . . . I'd be leaving you in the lurch, wouldn't I?'

He laughed gently. 'I'd be delighted for you. Nothing is set in stone and if circumstances change we'll change with them. Promise me you'll give the idea serious thought.'

'I will. I'll talk to the others and—'

'No, Olivia! You must make up your mind *before* you talk to them. They will naturally want you to stay in England because that will suit them. You can't blame them. They don't want to lose you but they have their lives and you have yours.'

Olivia nodded, wanting to be convinced. The idea, frightening as it was, was growing on her. Did she dare give up all that she knew and held dear, and go to California with Larry?

'I'm leaving for Liverpool for the ship's passage in two weeks' time – wait, Olivia!' He held up his hand to forestall any more arguments. 'I'll book my passage in three days' time and I'd like to book two cabins! What do you say?'

Olivia shut her eyes and took a deep breath. Knowing that if she spent too long considering the offer she would never agree to go. 'I'll do it!' she whispered.

1904! 20th July. Four years later!

After all this time I have found my missing diary, which I thought I had left behind at Laurel House, and will write a few last lines before abandoning it for ever. I've been rereading it and it seems that that life I had in England is more like a dream than my own past, and the last four years have flown so fast – but then a lot has happened. Larry says I now sound like an American although I cannot hear the difference myself.

It was very strange at first and for several months my life here was so alien that I secretly regretted my decision. But I had made my choice so I said nothing to Larry and gradually I became reconciled to my new lifestyle and now would not choose to go back to England. Having said that, there are a few days when the interminable Californian sunshine is too much and I long for some damp and blustery Kent weather . . . . !

Olivia paused, listening, then slid from the bed and made her way along the passage to the children's bedroom. As she expected, the younger boy Jon, aged five, was standing beside his bed, apparently wide awake but actually sleepwalking. Gently she took his hand and coaxed him back into the bed, settled him down and kissed him goodnight. She turned to seven-year-old Ben who still clutched a blue rabbit his mother had knitted for him years ago. When she was satisfied that they were both sleeping comfortably Olivia went back to her own bed, picked up her diary and continued.

. . . Our original plan was that I would live in Larry's hotel and learn all about the running of it but Fate intervened as it often does and I found myself acting as housekeeper to Larry's much younger cousin Donald. He was widowed shortly after I arrived when his wife caught diphtheria and was dead within a week. Thank the Lord the two boys survived . . . It must have been bad enough for Don to lose his wife that way.

Now Donald and I are married and I am Mrs Donald Kline (the wife of a chemist!) and a stepmother to the boys. I am possibly the happiest woman in California and my only regret is that my own family are so far away.

But they are thriving. Theo is working on his third book on antiques and he and Cicely have another child on the way. Bertie and Izzie have a little girl but Fenella (now Mrs Lucas Fratton) is too involved with running the gallery (which leaves Luke time to paint) and says she has no interest in producing any children!

Olivia allowed her thoughts to drift to Alice Redmond, who had been buried, at her own wish, in the small church in Newquay.

. . . The family went down to Cornwall with the exception of Theo, Cicely and Larry and we found ourselves part of a huge congregation which spoke volumes for the respect and affection in which Alice

had been held. Fenella accompanied the family as 'a family friend',
but two years later, after her divorce, she and Lucas were married in
the same church . . .

Not being at the wedding had caused Olivia some anguish
but they had been sent a wedding photograph which stood
on the table in the parlour with all her other mementos of
'home'.

Footsteps on the stairs now alerted her to the fact that her
husband was on his way to bed and she quickly hid the diary
under her pillow, put out the bedside light and pretended to
be half asleep.

Sitting on the edge of the bed Don began to tug off his
boots. He said, 'Are you asleep, Olly?' and Olivia smiled. This
was always the preamble to a late night exchange about when
to tell her family the truth.

'No,' she admitted, turning to smile at the familiar, well-
loved face of her husband. He was more dapper than his cousin,
more precise in some ways – Olivia put it down to his being
a chemist – but the family resemblance was there in the voice
and ready laugh, and it pleased her that the two men were
such good friends. Larry, still unmarried, was a regular visitor
and the two boys adored 'Uncle Larry'.

He said, 'Boys all right?'

'They're fine. Jon was out of bed fast asleep but he was just
standing there.'

'His mother did that as a child.'

'I guess it runs in the family.'

'Ben's never done it. Funny that.' He pulled off his shirt and
tossed it on to the nearest chair. 'I've been thinking,' he said
thoughtfully. 'Maybe you and Larry should bite the bullet and tell
them. You know. The family. Take a chance that they'll understand. What d'you think? I mean the longer you wait . . .'

She sat up a little and looked at him. Untidy fair hair flopped
round his good-natured face and his grey eyes were anxious.

'It's up to Larry,' she said. Her usual reply. 'It's his lie. He
has to deal with it. Not me.'

'You should have told them after Izzie's wedding.' He raised
his eyebrows. His usual argument.

'But we didn't.' She closed her eyes and yawned. 'I keep

telling you, Don. Everything happened so quickly. You can't hope to imagine what a mess we were in, one way and another. First Father turning up then Fenella leaving her husband and finally Aunt Alice dying! Disaster on disaster!'

Donald said, 'Still . . . Larry needs a push sometimes. He's always been that way. "Let sleeping dogs lie." That's Larry's motto. Always has been.'

'Not always. He did come to England to seek us out – and he did tell *me*.'

He climbed into bed, reached across and turned off the light. 'And four years have gone by!' He slid an arm round her. 'I'm glad he brought you back with him!'

'So am I!'

He kissed her and she crossed her fingers that the little homily was over. She was disappointed.

'Still, it's not right to keep the rest of the family in ignorance. They deserve to know the truth.'

Wistfully she said, 'But they may be quite happy *not* knowing. They may be happier. Maybe the belief that their father did come back to them is a great comfort.'

Already on the verge of sleep he muttered, 'Doesn't make it right!'

'Soon then,' she told him. 'I'll remind him. He's going to write a letter to Theo to share with the others.'

'He's been saying that for four years!'

'I'll give him a prod. I promise.' Olivia snuggled down next to him. Would Larry ever get up the courage to confess, she wondered. Would they be having this same conversation in ten years' time?

'You should, Olly,' Don murmured.

'Mmm.' She closed her eyes.

Five minutes later they were both asleep.